"To the Stars Through Difficulties"

Mortar and shells explode in the Po Valley in northern Italy during World War II. Frightened American soldiers dive into mortar craters and foxholes providing temporary cover from the shattering blasts.[1] Some die before making it to safety. A twenty-one-year-old United States Army second lieutenant named Bob Dole, who had led his high school basketball team to victory, now leads his men of I Company in an assault on a German machine-gun nest. His sergeant, Frank Carafa, provides covering fire. Dole's radioman moves out. He is hit. Dole grabs him and pulls him back into the foxhole. His young friend is dead, but there is no

time to mourn in the midst of gunfire. As Dole scrambles out again to help the rest of his men, he feels a sharp pain pierce his right shoulder. He collapses facedown in the Italian dust. He cannot feel his arms. He yells for help. Sergeant Carafa crawls over the rocky ground, grabs Dole's right arm, and drags him to safety. The rest of that fateful day of April 14, 1945, blurs in pain and morphine for Dole. The men of I Company, soon joined by the troops of K Company, take Hills 909 and 913. The mission is accomplished, but there are 462 wounded and 98 men killed.

• • • • •

On May 8, 1945, just three weeks after this attack, the war in Europe ended. Dole tried to keep his spirits up and hope for the best, but he also felt sorry for himself. "Why me?" he asked.[2] Had the war ended three weeks sooner, or had Lieutenant Robert Dole been only a few yards away, he would have escaped severe injury. But he had not been that lucky. He could not feel anything below his neck. His spinal cord was injured. Some doctors predicted he would never walk again.

Dole spent over three years in Army hospitals, making progress in small steps. He worked hard in physical therapy and learned once more how to eat, dress, and write. He did walk again. He could not use his right arm, but he learned to depend on his left.

It was a struggle, but with the support of family and friends and a compassionate surgeon, he learned

to think in terms of ability rather than disability. Bob Dole adopted a philosophy of "making the most of what you have."[3] He began to tell himself, ". . . maybe Bob Dole can do something else."[4]

As with many people who have suffered through war, Dole does not like to dwell on the experience. However, over the years he has reflected on what his war injury has meant in terms of his own growth as a human being.

> *Beginning the morning of April 14, 1945, I learned the value of adversity. A handicap can become an asset, I've since discovered, if it increases your sensitivity to others and gives you the resolve to tap whatever inner resources you have.*
>
> *Much of my life since April 1945 has been an exercise in compensation. Doors have been closed but windows opened. Maybe I couldn't use my hand, I told myself, but I could develop my mind . . . .[5]*

Bob Dole did develop his mind and persevered through hard times. He completed law school and advanced from county attorney to congressman to United States senator.

On April 14, 1969, on the twenty-fourth anniversary of his war injury, Bob Dole gave his first speech on the Senate floor. It was an appeal for an experimental housing program for the handicapped. Clutching a pen in his withered right fist, as he often does in public today, the forty-five-year-old senator spoke about the status and treatment of disabled

Americans, a topic that was not easily discussed in the late 1960s.

> *It is a group which no one joins by personal choice—a group whose requirements for membership are not based on age, sex, wealth, education, skin color, religious beliefs, political party, power, or prestige.*
>
> *As a minority, it has known exclusion—maybe not exclusion from the front of the bus, but perhaps from even climbing aboard it. . . . Maybe not [exclusion] from day-to-day life itself, but perhaps from an adequate opportunity to develop and contribute to his or her full capacity.*
>
> *It is a minority, yet a group to which at least one out of every five Americans belongs.*[6]

In his deep voice, Senator Dole urged his colleagues to help. "Our handicapped citizens are one of our nation's greatest unmet responsibilities and untapped resources. We must do better."[7]

Colleagues praised Dole for his speech, and Senator Norris Cotton from New Hampshire predicted for Dole "a long and distinguished career."[8]

Twenty-five years later, on April 14, 1994, President Bill Clinton dropped by Dole's office to praise the senator's continued efforts for the disabled. Clinton, who had taken the time to read Senator Dole's first speech of April 14, 1969, commented, "It was one of those magic moments in the history of Congress and maybe our country, which reminds us all, for all our differences, there's a common cord that unites us when we are all at our best."[9]

Bob Dole believes that every individual can make

a contribution to society if given a chance. Since Bob Dole's World War II injury over fifty years ago, he has served others through his work in government. He loves his home state of Kansas and its motto: *Ad Astra per Aspera* (to the stars through difficulties). These words have guided him through a distinguished and often difficult career.

Growing Up in Kansas

Robert Joseph Dole was born on July 22, 1923, to Doran and Bina (Bye-na) Talbott Dole in the small town of Russell, Kansas. Bob was named for his two grandfathers, Robert Dole and Joseph Talbott. The Doles already had a year-old baby girl named Gloria, and before the end of the 1920s, the family included Bob's younger brother, Kenny, and baby sister Norma Jean. The family of six all lived in a three-room home consisting of one bedroom, a living room, and a lean-to kitchen. The family used orange crates for shelves. They were not able to move into a larger house until Bob was nine.

Bob's paternal grandparents, Robert and Margaret Dole, were tenant farmers, farmers who did not own

the farms on which they lived. His maternal grand-parents, Joseph and Eva Talbott, farmed and butchered hogs and cattle and sold the meat to local grocers. Bob helped Grandfather Dole feed the chickens, gather eggs, and milk the cows. He helped Grandfather Talbott deliver the freshly butchered meat to market. He saw farmers succeed through hard work and determination.

Growing up on the flat plains of western Kansas, Bob Dole heard many stories. Forty-nine years before his birth, a shimmering cloud opened up during the scorching Kansas summer of 1874. Grasshoppers began to fall, one by one, and then thousands upon thousands poured out until these short-horned grasshoppers (known as locusts) coated the ground several inches thick. Startled Kansans batted the locusts from their faces and hands and watched helplessly as the ravenous creatures champed through corn, flowers, leaves, peaches, apples, and grapes. They stripped the vegetation clean.

As a young boy, Bob Dole listened to this story and others about his home state. He heard tales of the farmers' plight when dry spells, snowy blizzards, and prairie fires made their mark on the Kansas land.

Bob also saw farmers fail firsthand, sometimes from the unpredictable Kansas climate, other times from government action that was not always kind to the farmer. In later years, when he served in the United States Congress and the United States Senate thirteen hundred miles away in Washington, D.C., Bob remained sympathetic to farmers' problems.

Dwight David Eisenhower, the thirty-fourth

President of the United States and one of Bob Dole's heroes, said, "Any youngster who has the opportunity to spend his early youth in an enlightened rural area has been favored by fortune."[1] Bob Dole felt fortunate and wrote in his autobiography, "It [Kansas] is my home, my roots, and my constant source of strength."[2]

Learning to survive difficulties came from his parents, Doran and Bina Dole. They lived by the two rules they taught: "Money isn't everything" and "If it

Bob Dole posed with members of his fourth-grade class at Simpson School in Russell, Kansas. Bob is the second from the right in the back row.

is worth doing, it is worth doing right."[3] The Doles shared hard work, hard times, and a great deal of love.

After Doran Dole's restaurant business failed, he opened a cream and egg station where he earned about fifteen dollars a week selling eggs, milk, and cream that he purchased from local farmers. Years later he would operate a grain elevator. He always remembered his customers' names and told them jokes. He missed only one day of work in forty years. His days began at 5:00 A.M. and often ended at 11:00 P.M. Wearing freshly laundered overalls and work shirt, he swept the store and sidewalks in front of his business. Bob often helped his dad load heavy cans of sour cream onto the Union Pacific railroad cars bound for the East.

Bob observed that no matter how busy his dad was, he would still take the time to spend hours at the bedside of a sick friend. And when he earned extra cash, he spent it on ice cream for everyone. Bob remembers, "Dad shared everything with his family except his own troubles."[4]

Bina Dole made most of the family's clothes, and she transformed hand-me-downs into outfits for her children. She brought in extra income by giving sewing lessons on Saturdays and selling sewing machines door-to-door during the week. Young Bob or Kenny loaded the heavy-duty machines into the family car for her. When a neighbor died, she went door-to-door collecting money for flowers. Her favorite

advice to her children was, "Can't never could do nothing. Now get busy."[5]

Bina was also a perfectionist. Bob recalled that he could eat off her floors, and she was even known to wax the little wooden porch on their humble home.[6] Every night she washed the corduroy outfits that Bob and Kenny wore to school, and Gloria and Norma Jean wore skirts with pleats ironed to perfection. Bob has happy memories of his mother's Sunday dinners of fried chicken and gravy, fresh vegetables, and homemade ice cream with chocolate sauce. Every

Bob, Kenny, Norma Jean, and Gloria enjoy a break from their play time. The Dole children always looked out for one another.

July 22, a homemade angel food cake was ready for Bob's birthday.

Bob was close to his brother, Kenny. When Kenny was recovering from a childhood illness, Bob often led him to school by the hand. On crisp fall days, the brothers often walked behind their dad as he tracked down jackrabbits. In late spring, they dug up dandelions for neighbors for five cents a bushel. One winter day Bob, Kenny, Norma Jean, and Gloria sheared their white dog Spitzy, thinking they could use his fur to make gloves. Another time Bob, Kenny, and Gloria dangled a dead mouse in front of Norma Jean and chased her for several blocks.

Bob was six years old when the Great Depression began with the stock market crash of October 1929. During this tragic period in American history, several million people were out of work, factories cut down production, and business and industry ran out of funds. One of three families had no money coming in. People did without necessities; many waited in long bread lines for something to eat. Author James R. Dickenson, a Kansas native, wrote of the Depression's effect on the human spirit: "It was a deep humiliation for people who prided themselves on self-reliance."[7] Many Midwesterners lived on cottage cheese and cream. The Doles had it a little better than many, since Bob's father was able to bring chickens and cream home from his creamery.

As Bob grew up, he continually saw people caring about the difficulties of others and sharing what little they had. He saw farmers helping each other plow the fields if one finished before another. He remembered

that hobos coming through Russell were sure to get a sandwich or something else good to eat.

While the nation was still in the midst of the Depression, Bob Dole was heading into his teenage years. Kansas was besieged with dust storms so strong that the air tasted of grit, the feathers of white chickens became brown-stained, and machinery clogged up and became useless. These Dust Bowl storms of rolling black smoke made noon look like the middle of the night. Many feared the end of the world was near. School was let out early in anticipation of these storms that began with huge black clouds that promised rain but rained dirt instead of the long-awaited water.

For several years in the 1930s, there were over sixty of these storms per year. As a result of the persistent drought and numerous dust storms, some areas lost as much as five or six inches of topsoil. Many cattle died from ingesting dirt as they searched for food, and the dirt in their feed wore their teeth down to the gums. Farmers actually prayed that weeds would grow so the soil would not blow away.

Like hundreds of other families, Bob and his brother and sisters put wet towels and cloths at the bottom of doors and around windowsills to protect their home from the invasion of dust, but the powder still sifted in. They scooped dirt from rooms with wheat shovels. If Bob's sister Gloria left out a bowl of water overnight, it became a bowl of mud by morning. During one storm, Bob stood on Main Street in Russell and could not even see the marquee of the Dream Theater fifty feet away. He feared that the

whole town might disappear.[8] The dust storms also buried people and suffocated them. Children died from dust pneumonia. Mothers wrapped babies in wet sheets so they would not suffocate from the dirt in the air.

Times were also hard financially. In 1937, when Bob was fourteen, the six members of the Dole family moved into the concrete-floored basement of their home on the corner of Maple and Tenth in Russell, Kansas. They rented out the main floor of their home to an oil company to make ends meet. It was not until the 1940s that they got to move back upstairs, but young Bob Dole never complained.[9]

The Dole children all helped out around the house and took jobs to earn spending money. Gloria and Norma washed dishes and baby-sat. Bob and Kenny had paper routes, mowed lawns, shoveled snow, washed cars, raked leaves, and delivered handbills.

In between chores, jobs, and schoolwork, Bob enjoyed movies at Main Street's Dream Theater or Mecca Theater. He attended the Owl Show, a late-night show that cost a dime, and watched Hoot Gibson, a movie cowboy, at the Saturday matinee.

Television was not yet a part of American society. Instead, radio provided home entertainment. Bob often enjoyed the antics of Fibber McGee and Molly, Fred Allen, and Amos 'n' Andy. Voices, sound effects, and musical cues helped him imagine the scenes. He fondly remembers: "Sometimes at night I crept close to the set, turned the sound down low to avoid

As a junior high student, Bob Dole studied hard.

detection and listened to post-bedtime treats like *The Shadow*."[10]

One of the best spots on Main Street in Russell was Dawson's Drug Store, where Bob worked as a soda jerk for $2 a week and all the ice cream he could eat. Dressed in a crisp white shirt and cap and bow tie, Dole served milkshakes for fifteen cents, malts for twenty-five cents, and colas for only a nickel each. He dipped single and double ice cream cones for Russell's schoolchildren, oil field workers, lawyers, farmers, businesspeople, and families that packed into Dawson's. E. B. "Bub" Dawson, one of the owner's sons, remembers, "Everyone liked Bob, especially the girls. Although I must say he paid a lot less attention to them than they did to him."[11]

During harvest time, Bob took cold soda, compliments of Dawson's, to the farmers lined up for several blocks along Main Street as they waited in trucks to unload their wheat.

At Dawson's, Bob learned how to deal with the public and use humor to hold his ground. He learned the zingers—the famous one-liners—that are still his trademark today. Chet Dawson, another of Mr. Dawson's sons, teased one of the young employees: "Hey, kid, come over here. This man was clean-shaven when he came in and now he's got a one-inch beard waiting for you to wait on him."[12]

Bob did more than serve the customers. He gained nine pounds during his first two weeks on the job, and chocolate ice cream is still his favorite. Dole wrote, "For me, Dawson's was a place to make

friends, a marvelous listening post and a source of income, all rolled into one."[13]

At home, Doran Dole usually discussed sports, especially baseball. But politics was the hot topic at Dawson's. Amid coffee cups, ice cream dishes, and cigar smoke, Russell's citizens discussed the pros and cons of President Franklin D. Roosevelt's famous "fireside chats" (informal radio talks to the nation to win support for his new programs). They also gave their opinions on Kansas governor Alfred M. Landon's farm relief and unemployment relief programs and his failed 1936 election bid for President of the United States against President Franklin D. Roosevelt. Young Bob, who listened with interest, would one day become one of Kansas's most respected politicians.

Bob Dole's after-school and Saturday job at Dawson's did not interfere with his schoolwork. His parents saw to that. They never had the opportunity to finish high school, but they were determined that their children would. Bob was shy, but he was a serious student. His teachers believed in him and tried to draw him out of his shyness. His relatives also encouraged him. He remembers Aunt Mildred Dole offering to pay twenty-five cents for a perfectly spelled paper. "I accepted the bribe, and remain a stickler on the subject to this day."[14]

In high school, Bob Dole was elected to the National Honor Society. He was also elected president of Hi-Y, a Christian organization, and he served as sports editor of *The Pony Express*, the student newspaper at Russell High. The prankster came out again when he took a five-gallon drum of ice cream into his

journalism class, hoping to use it as a bribe to talk the teacher out of the scheduled test. At first, his teacher insisted, "We'll have to eat fast because we're still going to have that test." But Bob's plan did pay off—the teacher never gave the test, and the class ate the ice cream.[15]

At Russell High School, the handsome Dole earned letters in basketball, football, and track. He played guard in basketball, and his sister Gloria praised his rebounding and passing.[16] Dole was the type of player who watched the whole court. He had

Bob Dole, a member of the Russell Junior High basketball team, is on the left of the top row.

to know how the play would develop and then tried to make things happen. He was a leader on the court, offering encouragement: "Don't give up, guys. We're gonna get 'em." "We still got a chance. They can go sour."[17]

Bob's football jersey read number 78, and in his senior year, the Broncos, Russell High's football team, had a record of 9–0. Fellow team member Adolf Reisig admired Bob for his ability to catch a ball, for telling a joke to break the tension of a big game, and for possessing high standards.

Bob and Kenny Dole were ahead of their time with weightlifting. They had made weights by pouring concrete into metal cans to make concrete blocks fastened to the ends of a lead pipe.

In track, Dole ran the 440- and the 880-yard races

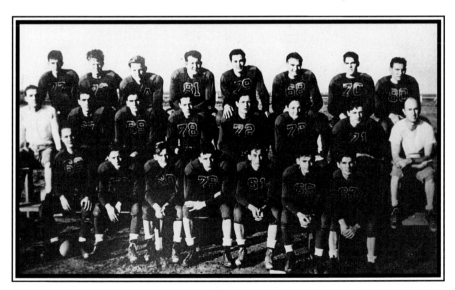

Bob Dole wears number 78 as a member of the 1940 Russell High School Union Pacific League Championship team.

well, but he also learned from other incidents that took place during some of his meets. He remembers seeing his friend Warren Cooksey, a powerful middle-distance African-American runner, being treated as a second-class citizen on the track circuit.

> *I was impressed by Warren's quiet dignity in the face of affronts. I was also angered at what seemed a blatant contradiction. If a man could be accepted on the running track for his talent alone, how could he be denied equal treatment in the race of life? I never understood how anyone could cheer for a black man on the basketball court but feel uncomfortable sitting beside him at a lunch counter.*[18]

During Bob Dole's last two years in high school, Adolf Hitler's conquests posed a serious threat in Europe. While German planes rained bombs from the sky and tanks plowed through country after country, most Americans were able to go about their normal daily routines. But the United States government kept a close eye on events in Europe and took certain steps to prepare for the possibility that the United States would enter the war. Its longtime ally Great Britain was in deep trouble as Hitler's bombs exploded on that nation's soil. Congress increased spending for America's national defense, and on September 16, 1940, the draft, a lottery that selects individuals for the armed services, was instituted. Before World War II's conclusion, Bob Dole would be involved in the fighting.

In June of 1941, Dole graduated from Russell High School during a time when most of western

Europe was under Adolf Hitler's control and America's relations with Japan were strained. Many Americans still felt the events were none of their business, but whether they were willing to support the war effort or not, the conflict in Europe was already helping to end the Great Depression that officially began in 1929. Many factories were in operation again, making materials to help America mobilize for war and sending aid abroad to countries ravaged by war.

War raged, but Bob Dole was thinking *medicine*. Two doctors who often came into Dawson's, Dr. Paul Koerber and Dr. Fagin White, influenced Bob Dole's career plans. He believed these two physicians made a great contribution to the community, and he liked the respect the doctors received. At Dawson's, their

Bob Dole leads on the outdoor track.

word was law.[19] "It was a short step from admiring doctors to wanting to be one myself," he recalled.[20]

Bob Dole was willing to put his college plans on hold if the financial burdens would be too much for his parents, but they managed to make the sacrifice.[21] In the fall of 1941, with $65 from them and a $300 loan he arranged on his own from George Deines, a Russell banker, Bob Dole became the first in his family to attend college. In order to earn spending money and help pay for his board, he waited tables at the fraternity for $12.50 per month and got up before dawn on Saturdays to deliver milk.

Bob Dole's humor and natural ability to lead made him very popular in college, and people liked to be around him. He enrolled in premedical courses and joined the Kappa Sigma fraternity at the University of Kansas at Lawrence. He was elected vice president of his fraternity. During pledge week, Dole played his biggest prank: He and a few friends carried a classmate's motorcycle to a third-floor bedroom.

Although not a starter, he made the university's freshman basketball team and proudly wore their red and blue. Dole played for the legendary Phog Allen, the father of modern basketball and future coach of Wilt Chamberlain. He also ran track and almost set an indoor record in the 440-yard sprint.

Several months into Dole's freshman year in college, the surprise attack on the United States' Pacific base at Pearl Harbor, Hawaii, took place on Sunday, December 7, 1941. More than twenty-three hundred lives were lost. America declared war on Japan as a

result. Suddenly, Americans were forced to realize that there could be an invasion of the West Coast. Attitudes toward involvement in the war changed. Some felt fear, but many wanted revenge.[22] Arguments about whether or not Americans should get involved in the business of Europe and Asia had almost vanished. By December 18, 1941, recruiting offices of both the Army and Navy were swamped. Many Americans went off to war—to a future no one could foresee.

The spring of 1942 brought many good-bye parties for friends who went off to war, and Bob wanted to be at the parties.[23] Bob's social life became more important than his grades, which soon slipped to the C range.

In December 1942, one year after the bombing of Pearl Harbor, Bob Dole made a decision that would change his life forever. Not waiting for the draft, he signed up for the Army's Enlisted Reserve Corps. He remembered: "I was nineteen years old, and eager to look life in the face."[24]

Preparing for War

Midway through his college career, the United States Army called Bob Dole into active duty.

During that summer of 1943, Dole entered basic training at Camp Barkley near Abilene, Texas. Dressed in their olive greens, Dole and other trainees learned how to take care of themselves and their weapons. Emphasis was placed on performing individual tasks and learning to work as one unit. In the future, these same skills would also help Dole lead and unite people of differing viewpoints in Congress.

After about six months of training in the Army Medical Corps, Dole was transferred to the Army Specialized Training Program at Brooklyn College in

Bob Dole was called to service in 1943.

New York City, where he studied engineering until March 1944. He enjoyed the new experience of a metropolitan area: Going to the top of the Empire State Building in Manhattan excited him, and he was fascinated by the mixture of races and cultures that were so different from life in rural Kansas.[1]

Soon he moved on to Louisiana and Kentucky. As part of the 290th Infantry, Dole learned how to operate artillery—guns so large they could not be carried and fired by hand but had to be mounted on a carriage, platform, or tank. He made the rank of corporal.

Dole was accepted into Officer Candidate School (OCS) at Fort Benning, Georgia, in the spring of 1944. While Dole trained to be an officer, Kansan Dwight D. Eisenhower led the famous D-Day invasion of Europe, helping turn the tide against Hitler in favor of the Allies—countries united against Hitler that included the major powers of France, Great Britain, the United States, and Russia. In the fall of that same year, Dole graduated as a second lieutenant. Before Christmas 1944, Dole was on a troopship headed for Italy, where he prepared to participate in the Italian Campaign phase of the war: German troops had retreated into the northern part of Italy, offering fierce resistance to the Allies.

In February of 1945, two months after his arrival in Italy, the Army assigned Dole to I Company, Third Battalion, 85th Regiment, Tenth Mountain Division. The division combined infantry, armor, and artillery as part of its striking forces. Replacing a lieutenant who had been killed, twenty-one-year-old Bob Dole

led a platoon in the Apennine Mountains in northern Italy. At this Italian location, the Allies intended to cut off a main supply route by attacking German fortifications in the hills and mountains around the Po Valley.

A month after Dole's arrival, a grenade fragment cut into his leg. He was patched up, awarded a Purple Heart (a medal awarded to any member of the armed forces wounded in action against the enemy), and returned to the front.

Lieutenant Dole became responsible for nearly fifty soldiers and was well liked by his men. Devereaux Jennings, who served directly under Dole, remembered, "He was always cool about things and very human. He never intimidated people or got outwardly tough. . . . He was the best officer I ever had."[2]

A lot of time was spent waiting. Trenches were dug, weapons cleaned, and areas patrolled. Dole wrote, "Men lay flat on their bellies for hours, peering through a twenty-power scope at enemy soldiers on a nearby ridge."[3] Artillery fire in the night made it difficult to sleep for those not assigned to patrol. Lonely soldiers waited for letters from home. Nervousness, uncertainty, and fear were constant companions.

As Lieutenant Dole listened to one of his men confide in him and tell him his doubts and fears, he realized that what this soldier had needed most was someone to talk to. Dole remembered, "After that morning, he no longer talked of cowardice, real or imagined. Small as it was, the incident taught me that listening can be a form of leadership."[4] Years later, being a good listener aided Dole's political career.

In the early days of April 1945, it was clear that Hitler's regime was about to collapse. Under heavy Allied air attacks and the assaults of the swift-moving armies, German resistance weakened. Lieutenant Dole and his buddies took bets on the date of surrender, and the Allied commanders planned strategies to make this surrender happen quickly.

One strategy, known as Operation Craftsman, was an Allied offensive created to take control away from the Germans in Italy. As the plan was set into motion, an event occurred on April 12, 1945, that saddened much of the world. President Franklin D. Roosevelt died of a cerebral hemorrhage. "The official announcement of his death listed his name as a war casualty along with others in the armed services who had given their lives that day. 'Army-Navy Dead: ROOSEVELT, Franklin D., Commander-in-Chief, wife, Mrs. Anna Eleanor Roosevelt, the White House.'"[5] The war was almost over, but Roosevelt did not live to see the end. And the troops began to wonder—would they?[6]

Vice President Harry S. Truman succeeded Roosevelt as commander-in-chief, and the business of war continued. Just two days later, tragedy would strike Bob Dole.

Dole and the 85th became a part of Operation Craftsman. Their orders were to take Hill 913 in northern Italy's Po Valley. Hundreds of men moved forward. For over thirty-five minutes, ear-splitting sounds of Allied P-47 fighter planes and explosions of 500-pound bombs dropped on Hill 913 echoed through the Italian hills. Smoke and machine-gun fire

filled the air. The Germans must be dead, the men thought. They did not know at this point that the Germans had been tipped off about the attack and hundreds of them waited for a fight.[7]

Dole's platoon moved forward, greeted by machine-gun fire, mortars, and artillery. Lieutenant Dole followed his order to take out the machine gunners holed up in a single stone house. The situation worsened as a mobile rocket launcher fired a large artillery shell toward the Americans. One of Dole's men recalled, "I was scared, I'll admit it. You have to be stupid not to be."[8] Grenades exploded. Another barrage of fire opened up. Soldiers scrambled toward the farmhouse.

Several members of Dole's platoon were gunned down. Others dove into mortar craters and foxholes. Dole remembers, "All around me, men were being hit. A combination of raw anger and protective instincts for my buddies took over."[9] When Dole's radioman was shot, Dole scrambled through mines and booby traps to get him, but he was dead. As Dole bellied forward once more to help his men, a bullet or exploding shell hit Dole's right shoulder. He could not feel his arms.

Dole called out Technical Sergeant Frank Carafa's name, Carafa related in an interview fifty years later:

> . . . *They were shooting all around. I had no intention of going out into that ravine, but then my men started saying, 'Sarge, get him,' and I couldn't lose face in front of them. I don't know what happened. I just kept going, kept crawling. I grabbed him by the right arm. He yelled and passed out. Then I dragged him back.*[10]

Carafa pulled Dole out of danger. Two medics were killed as they tried to get to Dole. Another sergeant, Stanley Kuschick, took morphine from a dead medic and administered it to Dole. With Dole's blood, Kuschick wrote the letter "M" on Dole's forehead as a warning to others not to give Dole another dose of morphine. It could have been fatal.

As Dole lay semiconscious, his hands crossed over his chest, machine-gun fire drowned out his moans. Dole's blood soaked into the dry earth beneath him, and visions of his parents, childhood friends, and his little white dog Spitzy flashed before his eyes. Dole's men continued with the fight. Assisted by backups from K Company, they took Hill 913 that afternoon.

Nine hours after his injury, Dole arrived at the 179th Evacuation Hospital, where many feared he would die. Dole could not move, and he had no feeling below his neck. At another hospital, doctors feared that if Dole lived, he would never walk again. They never told him there was no hope.

Two weeks after Dole was injured, German resistance in northern Italy finally collapsed. Italian partisans captured and killed Benito Mussolini, Italy's leader and Hitler's ally. The very next day the German forces in Italy surrendered. One day later Hitler killed himself as Russian forces bombarded the bunkers of his Berlin headquarters. On May 8, 1945, three weeks after Bob Dole was wounded, Germany surrendered to the Allied forces, and the war in Europe ended. Dole tried to be positive. He dictated a

letter to his parents because he could not use his hands:

Dear Mom and Dad,

I'm feeling pretty good today. I'm just a little nervous and restless, but I'll be okay before long. I'm getting so I can move my right arm a little and I can also move my legs. I seem to be improving every day and there isn't any reason why I shouldn't be as good as new before long.

Send me something to read and something to eat.

Love, Bob[11]

In early June 1945, six months after he had arrived in Italy, Bob Dole returned to America via hospital plane. "They shipped me back like a piece of furniture," he recalls.[12]

Although victory in Europe had been achieved, the war in the Pacific continued. Another campaign was to begin, and the homelands of Japan were to be invaded. Many soldiers who had fought in Europe received new orders to head for Japan. One soldier remembered, "I had a deep belief, right or wrong, that I would never come home again. I felt there was one bullet over there with my name on it. Too many of them had gone by me already."[13] Bob Dole was not able to move on to that campaign. The bullet that wounded him in Italy would have an impact on his life forever.

As fate would have it, victory in Japan was achieved before the November invasion plan had to be implemented. After the United States dropped two atomic bombs on Japan within three days of each

other, the Japanese official surrender was signed on September 2, 1945.

World War II took its toll in lives, property, and human suffering. Millions of men, women, and children had died. Millions more had suffered great hardships. Some may look in admiration upon the expert planning and brilliant strategies, but years later Bob Dole, who still finds it difficult to talk about his war experiences, believes, ". . . when all is said and done, war is infinitely more wasteful than glorious."[14]

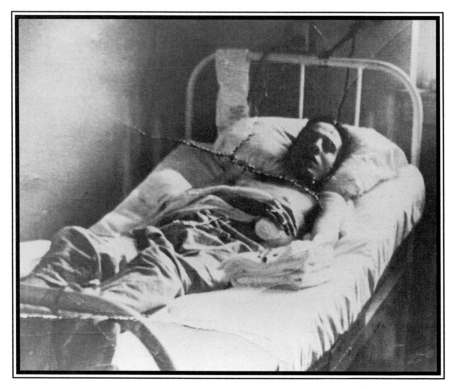

Bob Dole lies in a hospital bed after his World War II injury. His weight dropped from 194 to 122 pounds.

4

Hoping for a Miracle

For three long years, Bob Dole checked in and out of hospitals, trying to find a miracle that would make him whole again. When he first entered Winter General Hospital in Topeka, Kansas, his body was encased in a plaster cast from his ears to his hips. His mother, Bina, left their Russell home and rented an apartment to be by her son's bedside. She fed him, wiped his chin, washed him, read to him, and held cigarettes for him even though she was upset that he had started smoking, a habit he has since given up.

Whenever he came home to recuperate, his parents moved out of their first floor bedroom for Bob. His father read him the newspaper, and his mother

cooked his favorite meals. His brother and sisters were there for him, too.

That first Christmas after his son's war injury, Doran Dole traveled hundreds of miles to the Percy Jones Hospital in Battle Creek, Michigan, to be with his son. Through tears, Bob later recalled the gesture: "He had to stand all the way on the train. The trains were so crowded. He got up there—his ankles were so swollen. But he made it."[1]

During his long recovery period, Bob Dole rode an emotional roller coaster. When he made a little progress in his therapy, he convinced himself he would play basketball again.[2] Most of the time he tried to be upbeat, but it upset him to look at his shattered shoulder and withered right arm in the mirror. It would always be difficult for him to look in the mirror.[3]

Anger often took over. Sometimes a family member saw it on Dole's face when he could not complete even the most ordinary task—a task like bringing food from a plate to his mouth without dropping it.

Other times he learned to mask his feelings behind a wisecrack.[4] In the hospital, he told jokes and cheered patients. His good spirits amazed the nurses and doctors. They did not realize how he was really feeling.[5] His dream of being on the basketball court playing for Coach Phog Allen was being replaced by a vision of himself in a wheelchair selling pencils on Main Street.[6] Gradually he had to face the fact that he would never be what he had been.[7]

Bob Dole made more progress than the doctors first thought he would. About five months after the

injury, Dole moved his legs and gained some movement in his arms, too. When his full body cast came off, the young man who had once set the local record in the half mile now had to learn to walk all over again. Walking to the end of the hall gave him renewed hope.[8] When he fell, he tried to pick himself up so he would not have to depend on others. But he still needed assistance to feed himself, get dressed, comb his hair, and even go to the bathroom. His sister Gloria said, "He was pretty tough about it all. When he came home the first time, he didn't want help but needed it."[9]

Later Dole developed a special bond with others who have physical disabilities, and his experiences have taught him that physical wholeness is not a true measure of a person's abilities.[10]

In the 1940s, no ramps for the handicapped and special access to buildings were provided the way they are today. Since few quality jobs were made available for the disabled, physically challenged individuals feared being dependent upon the charity of others. Over thirty years later, Dole started the Dole Foundation, an organization whose mission is to promote economic independence for the physically challenged. Still in existence today, it provides more than $60 million in grants.

Dole remembers the first time he walked down Main Street to see his old friends at Dawson's Drug Store. He felt as if everyone was staring at him. "I felt that my disability was an embarrassment. My mood in those days was summed up in the tunes I played over and over on Dawson's jukebox. 'Laughing on the

Outside, Crying on the Inside' was one. 'You'll Never Walk Alone' was another."[11]

As a young boy, Bob Dole had taken pride in his physical accomplishments.[12] Now he worked hard at his physical therapy routine. He exercised to strengthen his legs, develop muscles in his left arm, and regain mobility in his hands. Some days he spent hours trying to close two fingers of his right hand. Wiggling a toe or bending a knee could be the most significant event of his day. He had to learn to eat and dress. Buttons created a problem, so Dole was happy to find Velcro, snaps, zippers, clip-on ties, and lace-less shoes.

Before the injury, Dole had written with his right hand. Afterward, he had to learn to use his left. Dole never regained full sensation in his left hand, and even today he needs more time than normal to write a few squiggly words that may be difficult for others to read. It is impossible for him to feel the difference between a quarter and a dime with his eyes closed, and he rarely loosens his tie, because it is a chore to knot it back up.

Bob Dole had hoped for a magic cure, but even at the Percy Jones Hospital, a place where amputees received new arms and legs and patients with spinal problems were often helped to walk again, he did not find one.[13] He left Percy Jones after months of therapy, without the strength to reach, push, or grab. But he left with the determination to cure himself.[14]

On another visit back home, Dole wore his old track shoes and walked around the neighborhood. On each walk, he tried to go longer and faster. He

squeezed a rubber ball in his left hand. He worked with ropes and pulley-weights that his brother and his friends hooked up on the garage wall.

Dole's high school friend Adolf Reisig worked in his body shop to design and build a special lead weight covered in felt to help Dole strengthen his arm. Dole wore that lead brace faithfully and soon took it back to Reisig, begging him to add more lead to be sure it continued to work. When Bob Dole's mom asked him to rest, he growled, "NO!" or ignored her.[15] One day the family found Bob trembling and perspiring as he hung from the garage rafters by only his bad right arm.

Despite many setbacks, Bob Dole still hoped for that miracle.[16] Dole thought he met his miracle worker in Dr. Hampar Kelikian, known as Dr. K, a pioneer in the surgical restoration of otherwise useless limbs. This small-framed doctor with gray, curly hair said that he could restore some mobility in Dole's arm and hands. The advice of Dr. K made an impression on Dole: "Don't think anymore about what you have lost. You have to think about what you have . . . and what you can do with it."[17]

Dr. K performed seven operations on Dole's right hand and arm. Dole described one of the procedures: "Taking a piece of muscle sheathing from my left leg, he reattached the arm as if threading a needle."[18] Dole did not get his miracle. He would never play ball again. The arm would not lift, but it began to look like an arm again. It began to look like a hand again. Dole gave it form by rolling his hand around a pen or folded paper to give it shape. Even today if he does not

control the arm, it hangs limply by his side, two and one-half inches shorter than his left arm. Dole cannot grasp objects with his right hand or carry anything heavier than a pen.

Nothing could restore what the war had blown away, and Dole began to accept his condition. He later wrote of Dr. K, "Even if he couldn't restore my right arm, he gave me something much more important: an example to live by, and a philosophy of making the most of what you have."[19]

Dr. K refused to charge Bob Dole for any of the operations, but the hospital bills following surgery had to be paid. Chet Dawson took an empty cigar box—a box Dole still treasures today—put a "Bob Dole Fund" label on it, and set it on the counter. People from Russell contributed dimes and dollars, eventually totaling $1,800, a lot of money in those days.

Between operations and therapy, Dole spent his free time watching movies, playing cards and chess, and reading. He and a fellow patient at Percy named George Radulescu created their own assignments. They studied wars, armies, great leaders, and the quality of leadership from the beginning of civilization to their present day: post–World War II. Dole came to admire George Washington's practical organization. Dole wrote of Abraham Lincoln, "His humble origins inspired me. So did the way personal tragedy only deepened his sensitivity."[20]

When their lessons were interrupted at 10:00 P.M. by a "lights out" order, Dole and Radulescu sneaked out of the hospital to a coffee shop across the street to talk about history until 2:00 A.M.

More happy events began to happen at Percy Jones. About three years after his war injury, Dole first noticed Phyllis Holden, an occupational therapist at Percy. She was attracted to him, too. A short time later they met at a dance. Unable to put his right arm around her back by himself, he put his arm on her hip, and they danced. They were comfortable with each other. His trademark sense of humor delighted her, and she did not want to date anyone else.

Bina Dole happily noted that most of Bob's conversations were now about Phyllis. He looked forward to driving to visit Phyllis and other friends in his specially equipped car, which he could drive with his left hand. Bob and Phyllis were soon married in June 1948.

Phyllis was tough with Bob and believed his family treated him too fragilely. "Do it yourself . . . you can do it," she would say to him.[21] She reminded him to do his exercises. "Pick up your feet, Bob," she said. "There's no reason to shuffle like that."[22]

In time she convinced his family that this tough approach was good for Bob. Bob realized it, too: "Phyllis made me forget my injuries. She helped me think, not in terms of disability, but of ability. She treated me like everyone else."[23]

Starting Over

Having accepted that the past could not be changed, Bob Dole focused on his future and set new goals for himself.[1]

With the help of the GI Bill student loan, a program designed to help service people gain an education, twenty-five-year-old Bob Dole enrolled in the liberal arts program at the University of Arizona in Tucson. Dole's veteran's disability pension and Phyllis's job as an occupational therapist helped them meet other expenses. Since his doctors recommended a warm, dry climate for his health, Bob and Phyllis had selected a school in Arizona. When he was not in class or studying, Dole jogged in the hills around Tucson. His legs and health improved. At this point in

his life, he tried hard to overcompensate for the time and physical ability he had lost.[2]

His college courses required a lot of note-taking, and even though Dole was at a disadvantage, he found new ways to succeed. Unable to write with his right hand, he wrote shorthand notes with his left. But writing was slow, so Dole began to memorize everything he could, including dates, definitions, and theories, repeating information over and over until it was stored in his memory. Before the war, his college days had been more carefree and social, but now his competitiveness drove him to study hard and master every subject.[3] One evening Phyllis, seeing his exhaustion, asked him, "Bob, why do you have to get an A? Why can't a C be good enough?"

"You tell me how to study a C or B's worth and I will. I can only study until I get it," he answered.[4]

After one year in Arizona, Dole made a decision to go to law school. In the fall of 1949, he enrolled in Washburn Municipal College (later known as Washburn University) in Topeka, Kansas, which offered him a joint program for an undergraduate degree in history and a graduate degree in law. He and Phyllis lived in an apartment across the street from the state Capitol. Dole remembers wearing a hole in the living room carpet "pacing around with a book in my hand, reciting the day's lessons."[5]

As Dole studied day and night to achieve his goals, Phyllis worked at the State Rehabilitation Center for the Blind and the Topeka State Hospital.

Dole used a Sound Scriber, one of the first recording machines manufactured. Small plastic records

inside a heavy box recorded the lecturer's voice. Before class, Dole plugged in the Sound Scriber, then he often worked through the night listening to the scratchy records over and over, slowly transcribing the information onto notepaper. Most professors made allowances and gave Dole his exams orally, but not everyone did. In those cases, Phyllis went to class with Bob and literally became his right arm. He dictated his answers to her, and she wrote them down. Later, when he took the Kansas bar exam, Phyllis was by his side. He had permission to whisper his answers to her.

One day Beth Bowers, a law librarian at Washburn, encouraged Dole and three of his classmates to enter politics. Dole remembers listening to Bowers:

> *It was a time for taking stock. I was never going to play football or wear a surgeon's gown. New ambitions sprang up in their place. It might take extra effort to achieve them, but that was no excuse to go home, rock on a porch and collect disability checks for the rest of my life.[6]*

Many townspeople of Russell already considered Dole a war hero and thought he would make a good candidate. While he was still in law school, Dole won election to the Kansas State Legislature in 1950 as a Republican. At age twenty-seven, he earned the distinction of being one of the youngest state representatives in Kansas's history. He earned only $5 a day and an additional $7 for expenses, but he still made sure he was present for all key votes and debates. Since the state legislature met for a total of

only three months during his two-year term, Dole managed to complete his studies while holding this political office.

In 1952, Dole graduated from Washburn and joined the law office of Eric E. "Doc" Smith. Soon the job of county attorney became available, and Bob wanted this political position. The job did not pay much, but it was a way to become established. In a high school gym, Bob Dole quickly announced his candidacy for county attorney in one sentence. He had bought a new blue suit on credit especially for this campaign. He liked to be a sharp dresser and took great pride in his appearance.

His campaigning began in the early morning hours and continued long after the sun went down. If Dole saw a light on in a farmhouse as he headed home, he stopped to introduce himself to the people inside. He passed out flyers on Main Street, and just as he worked hard at memorizing law cases, he worked hard at memorizing names and faces. He remembered:

> *Politics was a natural substitute for athletics. Knocking on a stranger's door, looking him in the eye and asking for his vote was a way to overcome my disability without denying it. Public service was also a way for me to give back a little of what had been showered on me by a generous community.* [7]

Dole won the primary battle for county attorney by 185 votes and continued his campaign to win the general election. One day he stood in the rain to greet Dwight D. Eisenhower, who had announced his run

for the presidency. In November 1952, as Bob Dole won a two-year term as county attorney by 2,142 votes, his hero Dwight D. Eisenhower was elected President of the United States.

Even though Bob Dole still worked in the private law practice, he became "the hardest-working county attorney Russell, Kansas, had ever seen."[8] He often worked past midnight taking care of the county's civil and legal business. He handled routine speeding tickets, minor crimes, and "driving while intoxicated" cases. At Christmas each year, Bob Dole and his brother, Kenny Dole, made sure that every needy child in town had presents under the tree.

One unpleasant task for Bob Dole as county attorney was signing welfare checks. This task was especially difficult since one check was made out to Robert and Margaret Dole, his grandparents, who had fallen on hard times. Dole agonized for the farm people who had worked so hard yet had not gained financial security.[9]

As he had done in law school, Dole followed a rigorous schedule. Still he made time for people, especially the Russell County farmers. He charged them low fees and helped them draw up wills and fill out license applications. In the spring, he did their tax returns for $2 or $3, or even for free. Many people learned that when Bob Dole told someone he would take care of the problem tomorrow, he really did.

Although Dole worked many weekends, he and his wife attended services on Sundays at the Methodist Church where he taught Sunday School. They enjoyed Sunday dinner with the Dole family, but

when work commitments came up, as they often did, Phyllis had to go to the dinners alone.

On October 18, 1954, Robin Dole, Bob and Phyllis's only child, was born. Dole said of that time, "Life was full, and full of promise."[10]

Dole served a total of eight years as county attorney, winning reelection in 1954, 1956, and 1958. He did this job well, but soon a new political prospect presented itself: The sixth congressional seat of Kansas became available. The winner would represent the 6th Congressional District in Washington, D.C.

Dole announced his candidacy for this Congress with theatrics: Twenty women known as the Bobolinks, dressed in red skirts and matching handbags, sang pep songs accompanied by a ukulele. A football player rode a tricycle, and a farmer wore an elephant's head, the symbol of the Republican party. Six men carried a coffin containing a Frankenstein dummy and a sign that said, "You have nothing to fear with Dole."[11] His daughter, Robin, who was then five years old, wore a skirt that read, "I'm for my Daddy—Are You?"

Later, when the Bobolinks became known as Dolls for Dole (a term that would not be used today), they wore matching skirts and striped tops sewn by his wife Phyllis and mother, Bina. They also wore white sombreros that featured the words "Bob Dole" in large letters under the brim.

Campaigning was different in the 1950s and 1960s. Then candidates basically told people who they were and what they intended to do and advertised a little on radio and television.

In the 1960 congressional race, Dole ran against two experienced opponents in the primary, Keith G. Sebelius and Phillip Doyle. Bob Dole worried that voters would confuse Doyle and Dole.[12] To make the distinction clear, Dole got permission to associate himself with the brand-name company Dole, a popular pineapple product distributor. His brother, Kenny, and other campaign volunteers passed out cups of pineapple juice to help voters remember Dole.

A small Conestoga wagon featuring the slogan "Roll with Dole" greeted prospective voters. Dole visited country stores, cafés, barbershops, filling stations, and five-and-ten-cent stores. While many politicians gave potential voters only a few seconds of their time, Dole often talked to people for as long as five or ten minutes. His left hand reached out to shake as many hands as he could. At public dinners, Dole felt uncomfortable about asking someone to help him cut up the food on his plate, so he began a practice that he still employs today. Instead of eating, Dole leaves the head table at dinners to mingle with the audience.[13]

After winning the primary, Dole ran against Democrat William A. Davis in the general election. Bob and Phyllis had to mortgage their home to help fund that campaign, but the sacrifice paid off.

On November 8, 1960, the day John Fitzgerald Kennedy was elected the thirty-fifth President of the United States, Bob Dole defeated candidate Davis by twenty thousand votes and would soon head to Washington, D.C., as a member of the United States Congress.

Dole's hero Dwight David Eisenhower extends a warm greeting to the newly elected Congressman in 1961.

The Republican Congressman in the Turbulent Sixties

Bob Dole sent his Aunt Mildred a picture of himself at the Capitol and wrote, "Finally made it. Lots of Democrats here."[1] And at that time in history, the Democrats controlled the White House, as well as the House and Senate.

At the historic House chamber of the Capitol, Bob Dole took the oath of office as a Republican member of the Eighty-seventh Congress's House of Representatives. It was the first time he represented Kansas's 6th Congressional District (later renumbered the 1st District) in Washington, D.C.

A little more than two weeks after he was sworn in as a congressman, Dole witnessed his first presidential inauguration. On the cold, sunny afternoon of

January 21, 1961, Democrat John Fitzgerald
Kennedy gave a brief inaugural address to the nation.
He concluded his inspirational speech with a call to
service. "My fellow Americans: ask not what your
country can do for you—ask what you can do for your
country."[2] Thirty-seven-year-old Bob Dole had
already asked and answered that question. Dole had
not come to Washington with the dream of being
President of the United States or even a senator. He
had come to Washington to be a Republican congressman and to make a difference.[3] Dole, who
admired Kennedy personally, would soon disagree
with many of his programs, labeling them too liberal
and too expensive.

During this decade when he had much to learn
about how government works, this dark-haired congressman from Kansas never lost sight of who he was
or where he came from. Although the power of
Washington politics and the privileges it often provided were magnetic to some, Dole was not affected by all
the attention. He felt embarrassed when someone
held an elevator for him or put him on the plane in
front of the other passengers.[4] Dole had even taken
the cigar box with him to Washington—the same cigar
box that the people of Russell had filled with contri-
butions for his recovery. The box would remind him
"of his roots and the compassion shown to him at a
very critical time in his life."[5]

Bob Dole was a hardworking congressman who
respected the voters back home. In the spirit of the
Kansas farmer and rancher who began their day early,
Dole was at his office by 7:00 A.M. He usually put in

fourteen-hour days, faithfully attending committee hearings, gathering important information, and being present when votes were taken.

Congressman Dole went out of his way to let his constituents know he cared. Every month he sent out a newsletter that he edited himself. He mailed certificates to all graduating high school seniors from his district and copies of *The Congressional Cookbook* to all future brides in his district. He spent many weekends on planes headed back to Kansas to cut a ribbon at a new store or speak at an American Legion Hall. In Washington, he often acted as tour guide for Kansas visitors, pointing out the large-scale historical paintings in the impressive rotunda or the stately House chamber in the South Wing of the Capitol. Sometimes Dole personally went to the White House to plead for White House tour passes so people from his congressional district would not be disappointed when they vacationed in Washington.

Since congressional staffs were small in those days, Dole read all his own mail. He dictated thousands of letters in reply and signed every one of them. Judy Harbaugh, Dole's secretary, held each letter for him to sign. One day he insisted on holding them himself by lifting his twisted right fist onto the corner of the letter to hold the paper. "There's so many things I can't do. I've got to try something every day, just to see if I can," Dole told Harbaugh.[6]

Larry Winn, a former congressional colleague of Dole's, remembered that Dole never got tired. "I'd say he's about as hard a worker as I've ever known in Congress."[7]

Dole's daughter, Robin, was very aware of her father's fast-paced schedule. As a teenager, she wrote her father a note requesting his permission to have her ears pierced. She listed all the arguments in favor and made a "yes" and a "no" box for him to check. Her father made a third box labeled "maybe," but he soon granted permission. Dole did make time to help Robin with her math homework and taught her how to drive a car. He also remembered Robin in special ways. Knowing that she loved the British rock group the Beatles, Bob Dole wrote to the British Embassy, hoping the Beatles would perform at Robin's high school. The Beatles were unable to accommodate the request, but her dad did get her to one of their concerts.

Congressman Dole also cared about the Kansas farmer and was fortunate to win a seat on the House Agriculture Committee. This committee, like others in Congress, had the power to introduce bills, hold hearings, conduct investigations, and oversee government programs. Over the years, Dole has earned the title of "one of the greatest friends that farmers have ever had" by battling for important issues, including rural development, environmental assistance programs, crop insurance, and the expansion of farm exports.[8]

In 1962, Dole presented a resolution that made Congress investigate the dealings of Billie Sol Estes, a friend of then Vice President Lyndon Johnson. Estes had received $8 million from the Department of Agriculture for storing 50 million bushels of grain. In the prestigious newspaper *The New York Times*, "Bob Dole, freshman from Kansas, made the case for the Republican Party, and the American Farmer."[9]

As part of his strong anti-Communist beliefs, Dole also questioned Kennedy's wisdom in selling American grain to Communist countries. At the time, the United States and the Soviet Union were engaged in a Cold War. It was a war not of battles, but of words and threats as these two superpowers struggled for power and influence in the world.[10] As Dole gained more experience, he began to realize that a world market was important for the American farmer, and he became a supporter of Kennedy's Food for Peace program.[11]

In between all his responsibilities as a congressman, Dole campaigned vigorously to remain in office. Dole won his first reelection to Congress on November 6, 1962.

In spite of their opposing views, the following year Dole mourned the death of John F. Kennedy, who was assassinated on November 22, 1963, in Dallas, Texas. Dole continued to disagree with the policies of Lyndon Baines Johnson, who succeeded John Kennedy as President.

But in 1964 Lyndon Johnson and the Democratic party were extremely popular. The United States enjoyed a strong economy, and the world situation was relatively peaceful. Dole, a Republican, had a hard time getting reelected in 1964. Shortly before the November election, Richard M. Nixon, the former vice president under Dwight D. Eisenhower, came to Dole's rescue. Nixon stood on bales of hay at a Kansas football field and delivered an impressive speech in Dole's behalf to over five thousand prospective voters. In that November 1964 election where Democrat

Lyndon B. Johnson won reelection as President with the largest popular vote in history, Republican Bob Dole narrowly won his own election against Democrat Bill Bork by 5,126 votes, just a little more than the number that had packed that football field. He was one of the few Republicans who had done well.

After the 1964 election, the Republican party weakened. They had lost some important elections, including thirty-eight seats in the House, where Democrats outnumbered the Republicans 295 to 140. Republican party members began to fight among themselves.

Remembering that his 1964 victory had been so close, Dole worked extra hard to win reelection again. Throughout all his campaigns for reelection to the House of Representatives, Dole continued to be a tireless campaigner. He told stories and jokes, made up speeches on the spot, and moved through the large crowds with ease, shaking hands and remembering people's names. He rarely had time to eat, but grabbed peanuts, colas, and chocolate milkshakes on the run. Seeing Bob Dole on the campaign trail often made one forget his disability, but his disability was still with him.[12] On a campaign morning, it might take him a half hour to button the top button of his shirt. Sometimes he had to tie his tie five times to get it just right. Dole won reelection in 1966 by over fifty thousand votes.

By 1966, the country was plagued by problems, and many Democrats were losing favor. The United States' involvement in the Vietnam War escalated, and inflation, partly caused by the war, was on the

minds of Congress and the nation. Race riots, brought on by decades of frustration among urban African Americans and other minorities over education, housing, and employment, occurred in many major cities throughout the nation. Since some Democrats also became discouraged with President Johnson's policies, Congressional Republicans now found new Democratic allies. Together they hampered Lyndon Johnson's Great Society programs of spending and social reform. Johnson's administration was rebuffed on every major bill it wanted signed into law.

Dole had spent much of his time in Congress keeping true to conservative Republican principles and voting against much of the Kennedy and Johnson proposals, including the bills establishing food stamps, Medicare, federal education assistance, and other programs designed to help the needy. Yet he did break from conservative ranks by voting for two very important pieces of legislation: the 1964 Civil Rights Act, in which Congress struck down racial barriers in the workplace and in public accommodations, and the 1965 Voting Rights Act, which ensured voting rights for African Americans. Dole explained, "I did so for sound conservative reasons. If American Conservatism stands for anything, it is the protection of individuals in all their rights, the right to vote being the most basic in any democracy."[13]

By 1967, dissatisfaction with the Johnson administration was at a new high. Many Americans resented the mounting costs of the Vietnam War, which soared to more than $2 billion a month. Viewers witnessed daily television coverage of fighting

in Vietnam. For the first time in history, Americans could turn on their television sets and see images of children crying, bloody body bags, and a daily tabulation of casualties from the war. Antiwar demonstrators picketed President Johnson. Higher prices and the expense of the President's Great Society programs troubled Americans, too. Racial tension grew, and in 1967 and 1968, the country witnessed the worst urban rioting in the twentieth century, where city blocks were burned to the ground and Americans of different races and beliefs turned against each other.

On March 31, 1968, amid great dissent and divisiveness, President Lyndon B. Johnson announced he would not run for reelection. A few days later, Dr. Martin Luther King, Jr., a civil rights leader who advocated brotherhood and nonviolence, was assassinated. Two months later, presidential hopeful and civil rights activist Senator Robert F. Kennedy, brother of John F. Kennedy, was also assassinated. America was losing its heroes, and the nation mourned and protested.

As the turbulent decade drew to a close, Bob Dole, who had served four terms as a Republican congressman, realized he did not have much clout in the House to significantly influence changes in policy. He set his sights on the Senate, which offered more power. "Why do something if you can't make a difference?" he reasoned.[14] As a United States senator, Dole could represent the entire state of Kansas instead of just one district. Plus he would only have to run for reelection every six years instead of

Bob Dole escorts his daughter, Robin, who represented Kansas as Cherry Blossom Princess in Washington, D.C.

every two, meaning less time on the campaign trail. When Frank Carlson, the distinguished senator from Kansas, announced his retirement from the Senate, Dole decided to seek his seat.

Once again Dole posters, buttons, and hats appeared on the scene. Voters were treated to white sheet cake and Dole pineapple juice. Dole won the coveted Senate seat.

On that same day of Dole's victory, in one of the closest elections of the century, Republican Richard M. Nixon defeated Democrat Hubert Humphrey and Independent George Wallace to become the thirty-seventh President of the United States.

As the last January of the 1960s arrived, forty-five-year-old Bob Dole was sworn in as a United States senator. Dole wrote a special note:

Dear Robin:

Today is a most important day in my life, and I trust in yours. The days and months ahead will be hectic, exciting ones, but my one hope is that I can share more time with you and your mother. In future years, as you look back, you might recall that my first letter after taking oath as a United States Senator, was written to you.

In the rush of today's activities, just remember that I always appreciate, more than you know or I can express, your patience, understanding, and devotion.

Love, Dad[15]

Even as an adult, Robin Dole still hit the campaign trail for her father.

Making Waves

As a freshman senator, Bob Dole became the self-appointed defender of President Richard Nixon. The six-foot-two-inch Kansan rose from his mahogany desk in the back row of the Senate to blast the Democrats who attacked the Nixon administration's handling of the Vietnam War. "Accusations that the President . . . has used the lives of our men in Vietnam as political pawns are the meanest and most offensive sort of political distortion," he stated.[1]

Dole also defended Nixon on his most controversial proposals, including construction of the Safeguard antiballistic missile system and two Supreme Court nominations. Some colleagues soon

referred to Dole as "Sheriff of the Senate"[2] and Republican "hatchet man."[3] Some liberal and moderate politicians resented Dole's "sharp tongue-lashings" directed at them because they dared to question Nixon's policies or approaches.[4]

Defending Nixon was not difficult for Bob Dole. Nixon's knowledge of politics and his strength and courage in overcoming obstacles impressed him.[5] Dole appreciated Nixon's gesture of always remembering to extend his left hand to Dole as well as the help Nixon had given him during a tough campaign.[6]

In addition to defending Nixon in the Senate, Dole also wanted to defend Nixon's policies from the broader platform as chairman of the Republican National

Dole meets with President Richard M. Nixon at the White House.

Committee (RNC).[7] Amid protests from some Republicans that Dole was "too aggressive and abrasive for the job," Nixon appointed Dole to the post.[8] As the Republican national chairman, Bob Dole toured the nation, building up the committee's finances, appealing to people who felt disenfranchised from the Republican party, and attacking television networks for what he considered their biased reporting of the Vietnam War.

Dole often worked seventeen-hour days, seven days a week. One of his aides said at the time, "As far as I know, the Senator has no hobbies. What he's most interested in is getting other Republicans elected and that's the way he spends his spare time."[9]

Dole hardly had time for his wife and daughter. Dole himself admitted that with a schedule like his it was hard to sustain a marriage. Dole reflected, "I was caught up in one life, whose demands were escalating, she [his wife] in another."[10] Phyllis remembered that politics was his main interest and that she and Robin did not see Bob often.[11]

In January 1972, Bob and Phyllis divorced. He moved into an apartment in the Watergate Hotel, a hotel/apartment/office complex located a few blocks from the White House. His mother, Bina, was crushed over the divorce and blamed her son. Bob had been raised to believe that "anyone who couldn't make a marriage work was a failure."[12] Some thought it hypocritical that while Dole worked on a welfare reform bill to strengthen families, he left a teenage

daughter and a wife who had been by his side during a difficult time in his life.[13]

Phyllis, who remained friends with Bob Dole, made him promise he would discuss the divorce with Robin, who was then a senior in high school. Robin credits both parents with making the divorce easier for her to deal with since they did not want their differences to hurt her.[14]

At that time, many people looked unfavorably on divorced politicians. Dole went to Nixon and offered to quit the RNC chairmanship if the divorce would embarrass Nixon or the party. Nixon reminded Dole that public and private lives should be judged separately.[15]

Dole stayed on as chairman, and Nixon prepared for reelection. But Dole "soon found to his dismay that the White House had shut him out of any decision-making role in the 1972 Presidential campaign."[16] When Dole approached Nixon at public events asking to meet with him, Nixon agreed, but Dole was never able to get through to Nixon to arrange these meetings. Dole explained, ". . . it was often impossible to penetrate the little circle that was rapidly becoming a noose around the President's neck."[17]

On June 17, 1972, an event took place that changed American politics forever. It would soon be known as Watergate. Five men, led by E. Howard Hunt, sometime spy novelist and CIA operative, were arrested for breaking into the Democratic National Committee headquarters in the Watergate office building in Washington, D.C. At first, it was viewed as

a simple office burglary and ignored by the public, but an investigation unveiled an elaborate scheme to bug Democratic National Headquarters and a cover-up that led all the way to the White House.

In the meantime, Nixon was far ahead of his opponent, Democratic presidential candidate Senator George McGovern, in the polls. The Republican National Committee (RNC) and the Committee to Reelect the President (CRP—Dole called it CREEP and the nickname stuck) worked hard to assure that Nixon did get reelected.[18] Both worked hard, but not together. Dole did not approve of the dirty tricks that CREEP wanted to play on some of the Democratic candidates, and he resented that CREEP seemed to have more of the money and the power. CREEP did not devote time and money to Republican senators and congressmen who needed to be elected or reelected.

Despite the tension between the two organizations, Richard Nixon won reelection by a landslide in 1972. But some Republican senators lost their seats to Democrats, and Dole criticized Nixon for not actively campaigning for them.

Usually the Republican party chairman is right behind the winning Republican candidate on inauguration day, but on Nixon's second inaugural day, January 20, 1973, Bob Dole and his daughter, Robin, were in the car at the end of the inaugural parade. CREEP had given Bob Dole the final snub.[19]

Two weeks after the election, Nixon asked Dole to step down as chairman of the Republican National Committee and gave the position to George Bush, who

sixteen years later would be elected president. Dole felt as if he had "been pushed off the mountain."[20] When Dole left the post of chairman in 1973, Senator George McGovern said of Dole's ouster, "I thought they treated him pretty shabbily in view of the fact that he seemed to do everything he could to be helpful."[21] Dole would not blame Nixon, but he did blame "a faceless nameless few in the White House . . . the gutless wonders who seem to take personal satisfaction in trying to do somebody in."[22]

The summer of 1973 was filled with the televised Watergate hearings. Some Americans watched the live coverage all day and the reruns of the testimony late at night. They were incensed by the intrigue, dirty tricks, and abuse of power. But Dole felt that the public was tired of the hearings and the matter should be settled in court.[23] Unaware of Nixon's involvement in a cover-up, Dole introduced an unsuccessful resolution in the Senate to end the hearings.

By July 1974, new evidence surfaced that Nixon was deeply involved in covering up the Watergate break-in and was guilty of obstruction of justice. Threats of impeachment brewed. Bob Dole, faced with this new evidence, stated on August 6, 1974, that the President's resignation "would be good for the party, but it would also be good for the country."[24] On August 8, 1974, Richard M. Nixon, facing pressure from all sides, became the first president in the nation's history to resign from the presidency. Vice President Gerald Ford succeeded Nixon. Ford announced, "Our long national nightmare is over."[25]

Just as the country began slowly to heal from the

trauma of Watergate, President Gerald Ford went on national television on September 8, 1974, and pardoned Richard Nixon for all the federal crimes he may have committed as president. Ford believed a trial that could take up to two years to complete would not be in the country's best interests.[26] Much of the country reacted negatively to this pardon, including Bob Dole.

Dole had to deal with whispers, rumors, and accusations of guilt-by-association in the Watergate scandal. Since Dole had been Republican National Committee chairman at the time of the Watergate break-in, many believed that Dole either had known about the break-in before it happened or that he should have known.[27] But Senate Watergate Committee chairman Sam Ervin exonerated both Dole and the Republican National Committee of any Watergate involvement. Senator Howard Baker commented, "That's sort of remarkable, considering the party positions he [Dole] held. He is absolutely free of taint."[28]

Not all voters paid attention to these statements of Dole's innocence, so he and many Republicans engaged in uphill campaigns in 1974. One of Dole's 1974 campaign flyers included the following quotation printed above two pictures: "You can sum up Senator Bob Dole with a 4-letter word: GUTS." One photo showed a close-up of Dole's disabled hand and the other a full-front picture of Bob Dole. Campaigners passed out hundreds of thousands of these fliers. After a series of nasty campaign ads, which Dole insisted did not have his stamp of

approval, he came from behind in a tough race and defeated Bill Roy, a two-term congressman, by a slim margin.[29] Dole would return to Washington for another six-year term.

During that difficult campaign of 1974, Dole often called Elizabeth Hanford, a friend whose ability to listen and offer encouragement made him feel better.[30] Dole had met Hanford, a Harvard Law School graduate, after his divorce. At the time, she worked as an assistant to Virginia Knauer, the White House advisor on consumer affairs. Hanford needed to speak to the RNC chairman about getting a consumer plank in that year's Republican party platform that would clearly state the party's position on consumer rights issues. Elizabeth thought to herself, "My goodness, he's an attractive man."[31] Although Dole wrote her name on his desk blotter after their meeting, months passed before he got up the nerve and invited her to dinner. Dole worried because he was thirteen years older than she was, but as he recalls, "I saw in her a genuineness and a sensitivity to others that are rare in power-hungry Washington."[32] After the two began dating, Dole's staffers noticed their boss whistling around the office, and he stopped calling them with work assignments every weekend. Bob Dole and Elizabeth Hanford discovered they had many interests and friends in common, including a strong devotion to public service. Dole quipped, "(A) we like to work, (B) we like to work, and (C) we like to work."[33]

Elizabeth's family accepted and admired Bob Dole. Elizabeth recalls one visit where Bob came down to breakfast wearing a towel over his damaged right

shoulder. As he pulled off the towel, he said to Elizabeth's mother, "Mrs. Hanford, I think you ought to see my problem."

Mrs. Hanford replied, "Bob, that's not a problem. That's a badge of honor."[34]

On December 6, 1975, Bob, fifty-two, married Elizabeth Hanford, thirty-nine, in a small private ceremony in the Bethlehem Chapel of the Washington Cathedral. Elizabeth wore an ivory satin wedding gown and a long lace mantilla. She had studied her vows before the ceremony. Bob had not rehearsed. He said "I do" before he was supposed to, but still it was a happy day. Robin Dole said of his father's new wife, "One of the things that I find very important and very special is that she never made an attempt to be my mother. I had a mother. Her effort was to be my friend."[35] The couple's honeymoon was cut short when they received news that Bob Dole's father, Doran, had died of a heart attack.

In 1976, America celebrated her two-hundredth birthday. Gerald Ford won the Republican nomination for president over the challenge from Ronald Reagan. On August 19, 1976, the day that would have been Doran Dole's seventh-sixth birthday, Gerald Ford asked Bob Dole to be his running mate. "I'm proud to do it," Dole answered.[36] Secret Service agents quickly arrived on the scene to protect the Doles and gave Bob and Elizabeth the code names of "Ramrod" and "Rainbow."

In Dole's acceptance speech, he said, "America wasn't built by men and women with limited vision

and small hopes and low expectations. It was built by men and women with tomorrow on their minds."[37]

President Ford launched his campaign against the Democratic ticket of Jimmy Carter and Walter Mondale in Dole's hometown of Russell, Kansas. The Dream Theater marquee, still there from Dole's boyhood, now read "Welcome President Ford and Bob."[38] On that sunny August day, amid the cheering crowds, including farmers in pickup trucks, Bob Dole spoke from the heart.

I never believed I would ever be in this position. . . . But it shows you can come from a small town in America and you don't need all the wealth and the

Bob and Elizabeth Dole arrive in Russell, Kansas, with President Ford after Dole signed on as Ford's running mate for the 1976 presidential election.

material things in this world to succeed . . . if I've done anything it's because of the people I've known up and down Main Street. . . . And I can recall the time when I needed help, the people of Russell helped . . .[39]

Dole stopped. The crowd grew silent as he covered his face with his left hand. Bob Dole cried so hard his shoulders shook. Some members of the crowd began to clap and cheer. President Ford stood up and applauded. The cheering continued. Dole gained his composure and thanked the people of Russell.

Elizabeth temporarily left her post at the Federal Trade Commission to campaign for her husband, and they were both tireless campaigners.

Dole told voters how Ford had restored trust in government and had already reduced unemployment. He spoke of Ford's plans to improve the economy and Ford's opposition to amnesty for draft evaders of the Vietnam War. He criticized the Democratic ticket of Carter and Mondale for wanting to raise taxes and make severe cuts in defense spending.

In a debate with Democratic vice-presidential candidate Walter Mondale, which was heard or seen by over 85 million people, Dole referred to Vietnam, World War I, and World War II as "Democrat wars." Authors Edward and Fredrick Schapsmeir later wrote, "Dole while trying to pin the blame for the Vietnam War on the Democrats, made the offhand (but factually correct) remark that Democratic presidents always seemed to be in office when the nation was involved in war (i.e., Wilson, FDR, Truman, and LBJ)."[40]

Dole greets one of the many crowds that gathered to see him.

Although Ford and others praised Dole's overall debate performance, many criticized Dole for his comments. Accusing the Democrats of being the "war party" and responsible for the deaths of 1.6 million soldiers did not go over well. Many veterans and families of war victims were offended. "Dole bombed out by coming across on the TV screen as excessively brusque and too flippant."[41] Even to this day, some voters only remember Dole's one remark. Almost twenty years later, Dole admitted, "I made a mistake. I shouldn't have said that."[42]

Despite the criticism, Dole and Ford campaigned on, and as the November 1976 election approached, polls indicated a close race. Ford and Dole had come

from 33 points behind, but right before the election, headlines reported the economy had weakened and polls revealed voters were still annoyed with Ford for pardoning Nixon. The Carter-Mondale ticket defeated the Ford-Dole ticket 51 percent to 48 percent. Dole had never lost an election before.

The next day Bob Dole was sick with the flu and campaign fatigue. While some of the media blamed Dole for Ford's loss, James Baker III, a top strategist for Ford, said, "I don't think you can say that Bob did anything but help the ticket. He was an indefatigable campaigner. And he certainly did everything the president and the campaign asked of him."[43] Elizabeth remembers Bob telling her, "I couldn't have gotten

Bob Dole and President Ford await election returns in 1976.

through this without you. . . . Now there's just one thing for me to do, and that's go back and be the best United States Senator I can."[44]

With Jimmy Carter's inauguration, Bob Dole began serving under his third president as a United States senator. Still he made more waves. Dole criticized Carter's energy plan for being very harsh on the poor, and during the first years of the Carter administration, Dole led the opposition to the Panama Canal Treaties. Dole proposed a catastrophic-health insurance program and introduced a plan to help American families save for their children's education with the help of federal tax credits.

As a senator, Dole created "working alliances" with both Democrats and Republicans. He learned that he could be close friends with individuals he differed with politically, including Democrat Hubert Humphrey, former vice president and presidential candidate. Dole also worked side by side with Democrat George McGovern on the Senate's Nutrition and Human Needs Committee, which studies and investigates the poverty and hunger in the United States.

McGovern credits Dole:

He got really caught up in that committee and he and I started working closely together on strategy for how to get legislation passed . . . it was a major expansion of the school lunch program and creation of the Women, Infants and Children Program, which Dole and I pushed through the committee and onto the Senate floor for passage in 1974. We conducted field hearings all over the country. We saw genuinely

hungry people and undernourished kids, malnourished mothers and nursing mothers and pregnant mothers, and we saw the ramifications for that in underweight children and for the learning process.[45]

In the later part of the 1970s voters saw a different Bob Dole. After the loss of the 1976 election, Dole, with encouragement from Elizabeth, began to work on his public image and speaking style. New York City speech consultant Dorothy Sarnoff advised Dole to project a take-charge attitude and show enthusiasm and concern. Sarnoff suggested Dole wear more dark suits and work on facial animation so he would not appear angry. She told him to stop leaning on his left arm. Instead, he should let his fingertips touch the edge of the podium and stand up straight.[46] Dole began to poke fun at himself. When asked how he took his defeat as Ford's running mate, Dole quipped, "On election night, I slept like a baby; every two hours, I woke up and cried!"[47]

On May 14, 1979, in his hometown of Russell, Kansas, Dole officially announced his first bid for the presidency of the United States. He told the crowd of about five thousand that the federal government had become too large. It needed to regain its focus of doing the compassionate thing and helping others. He invited Republicans and Democrats of all backgrounds and interests to join him in his vision of letting "America be America again."[48] Elizabeth resigned her job at the Federal Trade Commission to campaign for her husband. Dole tried to run a positive campaign and use his sense of humor to attract voters.

But many voters would not accept the "New Bob Dole." They remembered the old abrasive Bob Dole. As a result, little money filtered into his campaign. Dole could not campaign as much as he wanted because of his Senate duties. Daytime, he battled on the Senate floor to get an important bill through. At night, he flew to New Hampshire for a political event. The next morning he was back on the Senate floor. Dole saw himself as a working candidate with real experience, and he thought voters should admire that, but political observers concluded that Dole did not really want to be president.[49]

As the decade came to a close, Dole was still a candidate for the highest office of the land, but his prospects did not look good.

"Nothing Gold Can Stay"

In the early months of 1980, after a series of poor showings in presidential primaries and a disorganized presidential campaign, Bob Dole realized it was not his time to be President of the United States.[1] It was Ronald Reagan's.

Weary of politics, Dole even considered retiring from the Senate and taking a high-paying job with a prestigious Washington law firm, but he could not walk away from Capitol Hill. He still wanted to be a "player" in the Senate.[2]

November 1980 brought hope and renewal to the Republican party and Bob Dole. Reagan was elected President, and Dole enjoyed his twelfth political victory by winning reelection to the United States Senate.

For the first time in twenty-five years, the Republicans ruled the Senate by a majority of 53 to 47. This event was a milestone for Dole and the Republicans, for the majority party has the chance to initiate programs and line up the votes for their passage. Ronald Reagan appointed Elizabeth Dole secretary of transportation.

Dole soon earned the chairmanship of the powerful Senate Finance Committee, the main committee that handles taxes and Social Security and watches over almost half of the federal budget. Now he had the opportunity to work on the "truly towering issues facing America."[3]

Remembering firsthand how people suffered from debt,[4] he understood that people cannot continually spend more than they take in.[5] For years that is what the government had done, and the debt climbed higher and higher. Bob Dole took the unpopular stand of raising taxes to help reduce the federal deficit.

Dole led the fight for TEFRA, the Tax Equity and Fiscal Responsibility Act of 1982, which lowered the federal deficit by nearly $100 billion and raised taxes. At the time, TEFRA was the largest single tax-raising measure in United States history. The business community and conservative Republicans were surprised and upset with Dole.[6] Some fellow Republicans labeled Dole what they felt to be a very negative label of "liberal."[7]

When Dole was warned not to talk about another tax increase package in October of 1983, he went ahead anyway. He believed it was for the good of the

country.[8] He felt strongly that the price of leadership often required taking risky stands.[9]

Praise came Dole's way for this bold leadership on the economy, Social Security, and programs for the disadvantaged. Political analysts Rowland Evans and Bob Novak wrote, "Dole's record as chairman of the Senate Finance Committee is awesome. . . . Only a year after taking over the Finance Committee in 1981, he was shaping rather than following Administration fiscal strategy."[10]

Soon Dole gained a reputation as a problem solver and a compromiser, skills he had honed since his early days in Russell. Sometimes, to move good legislation forward, he had to give something up. Dole later stated, "I know that's a bad word to some people. 'Oh. Bob Dole, he'll compromise. He'll make a deal.' Well, in my view, that's not a fault. You retain your principles and try to work something out."[11]

In 1983, Dole supported the bill that made Dr. Martin Luther King, Jr.'s birthday a federal holiday. He opposed those who said Dr. King was too controversial or that a new federal holiday would be too expensive.

Dole reminded his colleagues, "A nation defines itself . . . in the promises it makes and the programs it enacts, the dreams it enshrines or the doors it slams shut. . . . Thanks to Dr. King . . . America wrote new laws to strike down old barriers."[12]

Even though Dole had argued with Reagan over tax policies, he supported Reagan against the Democratic ticket of Walter Mondale and Geraldine

Ferraro in Reagan's 1984 reelection bid. Reagan was reelected by a landslide, claiming electoral votes in forty-nine out of the fifty states. The Republicans remained in control of the Senate.

Bob Dole wanted to be Senate majority leader, the elected spokesperson on the Senate floor for the party that has the majority of seats. He campaigned hard for this position, which would make him responsible for enacting his party's programs. Optimistic about his chances, Elizabeth and Robin brought him a

President Ronald Reagan greets Elizabeth and Bob Dole on January 20, 1985, on the day of Reagan's swearing-in as President for his second term.

miniature Schnauzer from the Washington Humane Society and hung a sign—"Leader"—around the dog's neck. They were right. Dole won out over four other candidates, becoming one of the most powerful leaders in American government. As Senate Republican leader, Dole had a job in which "he had vindicated himself after two humiliating experiences in presidential politics."[13]

In defining his role, Dole wrote, "Any Majority Leader is part ringmaster and part traffic cop. He is an architect, building a legislative house brick by brick, commitment by commitment. Most of all, he's a juggler, keeping half a dozen balls in the air while looking down the road to see where vectors of policy and politics converge."[14]

One former aide to Dole described it differently: "Dole buttonholed his colleagues in countless cloak-room caucuses and used all his powers to coax, wheedle, and harangue them. Dole cut deals in which money was restored to senators' favored pet programs in exchange for their votes."[15]

As majority leader, Dole spent his long days "planning, pleading, maneuvering and politicking."[16] He worked endless hours keeping informed on both national and international problems and trying to find practical solutions. He met with President Reagan to discuss upcoming bills, and he scheduled legislation. Columnists Evans and Novak observed, "Not since Lyndon Johnson has Capitol Hill seen anything like the political skill and tenacity of the shrewd, tart-tongued Senator from Kansas."[17] Dole

received a lot of media attention but helped his colleagues get in the spotlight, too.

Even as Dole was chauffeured to work (a government perk of being Senate leader), he read the *Washington Post* en route. His days were filled with skimming newspapers, reading memos, signing mail, conducting news conferences, and speaking to groups, including the Disabled Veterans. In between, he met with other senators and advisors to discuss and focus on the goal of addressing the federal deficit.

Leader often accompanied Senator Dole to work.

At one point, he arranged over one hundred meetings to accomplish this goal.

Elizabeth Dole also had a full schedule with her job as a member of Reagan's cabinet as secretary of transportation. Despite their hectic lifestyle, they tried to make Sundays relaxing, attending church, enjoying brunch with friends, or reading the Sunday papers.

Amid praise and success, sadness again touched his life. On July 27, 1983, on the Senate floor, Bob Dole honored Dr. Hampar Kelikian (Dr. K), who had died at the age of eighty-four. Richard Norton Smith, one of Dole's talented speechwriters, wrote the eulogy. Woven into the speech was Robert Frost's "Nothing Gold Can Stay," a short poem that expresses the universal feeling of loss that time brings to all of us through nature's changes. As Dole delivered this tribute in honor of the doctor who had performed the expert surgery on his arm almost forty years earlier, emotion overtook him. He began to cry. Placing his speech down, he turned and walked off the Senate floor.

Within two months, Dole's beloved mother, Bina, died. He had called her almost every week of his life. Once, when President Reagan wanted to thank Bob for his support in the Senate, all Dole asked was that Reagan call his mother, who was in the hospital. President Reagan promptly obliged. The advice Dole's mother had given Dole during his boyhood, "Can't never could do nothing. Now get busy," helped him cope with loss once more.[18]

Despite personal losses, Dole feverishly worked to

get a one-vote majority to pass a budget that included a freeze on Social Security cost-of-living increases. He even called California Senator Peter Wilson's doctors to inquire whether the senator, who was still hospitalized from his emergency appendectomy, could make an important vote. After midnight on May 10, 1985, attendants wheeled Wilson to the Senate Chamber. Wilson, wearing his robe and pajamas and hooked up to an IV (intravenous) tube, answered "aye" to tie the crucial vote 49–49. Then Vice President George Bush broke the tie, and Dole's package won 50–49.

Dole's victory was short-lived. Later, a separate deal destroyed this Senate plan that would have saved the government $135 billion.

Even though this battle ended unhappily for Dole, he forged on to help the farmer by pushing the 1985 Farm Bill through. This bill, which increased farm subsidies, helped some farmers but added to the federal deficit. Dole defended the cost. "If you don't eat, you don't need to worry about the farmer. Otherwise, his problems are at least in part your problems."[19]

In November 1986, Dole won his fourth Senate term, but Republicans had a poor showing. Democrats regained control as the balance of power shifted in the Senate and fifty-five Democrats outnumbered the forty-five Republicans. Once again Dole considered retiring from the Senate and focusing on the 1988 presidential election. But then, the Iran-*contra* scandal hit the airwaves. Dole felt he was needed in the Senate: He defended President Reagan's lack of knowledge of this secret deal that involved the

United States government's selling arms to Iran and illegally diverting aid to the Nicaraguan *contras*.[20] Dole stayed and colleagues elected him minority leader on November 20, 1986. As a member of the 100th Congress, he supported the President and criticized the Democrats.

Ronald Reagan's second term as President would soon be up, and the Republicans needed a candidate. On a cold November morning in Russell, Kansas, in 1987, Bob Dole announced his second candidacy for the presidency of the United States. His hometown rallied around him once more. The high school Bronco Pops Choir sang "Twist and Shout," cheerleaders chanted, "Go, Bob, Go," and children waved tiny flags. Dean Banker's store featured a sign: "BOB DOLE SUITED UP HERE FIRST." Banners proclaiming "IT ALL BEGAN IN RUSSELL" decorated Main Street. Dole's ex-wife, Phyllis, sent handmade wooden buttons that read "DOLE '88."

Bob, with Elizabeth and Robin at his side, told the crowd, "I offer a willingness to work hard, to hang tough, to go the distance . . ."[21]

This time, Bub Dawson, whose brother Chet had started a fund drive for Dole after World War II, handed Dole a cigar box filled with $135,000 from the people of Russell for his campaign.

Amid the loyalty of Russell, victory seemed promising. But trouble hit his campaign as it edged outward to touch the nation's voters: It seemed that many of Dole's advisors spent more time fighting among themselves than trying to defeat George Bush.

In addition, Dole did not feel comfortable trusting his advisors to make decisions.[22]

Critics accused Dole of not having a vision, a theme for his campaign. But Dole felt he was skilled at getting things done and solving problems. He believed he offered voters "a vision of his own past: his wartime heroism, his many years in Congress, his service as the Senate's majority leader and currently minority leader."[23]

Nothing had come easily for Bob Dole, "not money, not position, not life itself,"[24] and he had a tough time accepting how easily things seemed to go for his major opponent, George Bush. Dole saw Bush as "a

Bub Dawson and Bob Dole admire the symbolic cigar box that represents the devotion of the people of Russell.

soft, untested man who had coasted through life on his family's wealth, his Ivied pedigree and his establishment connections."[25]

Elizabeth resigned as transportation secretary to help her husband once again. She was always well prepared for every speech she gave and charmed many voters with her warmth and soft North Carolina drawl.

Although Dole won the Iowa caucuses on February 8, 1988, with 37 percent of the vote, only eight days later he lost a crucial primary in New Hampshire. The Bush campaign had aired ads in New Hampshire attacking Dole, and Dole and his advisors had not fought back. Dole differed with Bush on the deficit, and when publicly put on the spot by Pierre (Pete) DuPont, another Republican candidate, Dole refused to sign a pledge saying he would not raise taxes. Some analysts believed this refusal doomed Dole's campaign. George Bush did sign the pledge, but later, during his presidency, he raised taxes anyway.

Dole was cast in a bad light when NBC-TV's Tom Brokaw asked Dole if he had any messages for George Bush after the New Hampshire loss. Unaware he was on the air,[26] Dole snarled, "Yeah, stop lying about my record."[27] The national media replayed that videotape of Dole's response, and critics announced that Dole's "mean streak" had returned.[28] These words haunted him just as "Democrat Wars" had in the 1976 campaign.

Dole lost every one of the seventeen "Super Tuesday" primaries, and he soon pulled out of the

race. As the presidency eluded him once more, he became "angry and withdrawn."[29] But Bob Dole had coped with the pain of loss before. After coming to terms with the fact that it was George Bush's time to be president, and not his, Dole sent his staff to find out what he could do for Bush's campaign. Characteristic of his loyalty to the Republican party, Dole campaigned for Bush. Both men put the bitterness of the campaign behind them.

When Bush defeated Michael Dukakis in 1988, he became the nation's forty-first president. Bush appointed Elizabeth Dole as secretary of labor, the only woman in Bush's original cabinet, where she served as the President's chief advisor in labor and work force issues. Bob Dole remained loyal to Bush throughout his presidency and voted in support of his policies almost 90 percent of the time. Dole worked hard in the Senate for passage of the Americans with Disabilities Act (ADA), a bill that protects the civil rights of disabled people.

Bush later wrote of Dole, "My respect for his leadership knows no bounds."[30] Dole often headed off Democratic attacks directed against Bush. He also lined up support of Republican senators during crucial situations, including the time of Desert Storm, when the United States was at war to liberate Kuwait from neighboring Iraq under Sadam Hussein. Bob Dole became one of the few people that George Bush felt he could turn to, a man "who would not waver and who had stuck with him."[31]

At the end of 1991, Dole, age sixty-eight, was diagnosed with prostate cancer, the most widespread

cancer among men in America. Doctors at Walter
Reed Medical Center performed three hours of cancer
surgery on Dole and removed his prostate gland. Dole
dealt courageously with prostate cancer and freely
spoke about his ordeal. He encouraged men over
forty to take the PSA (Prostate Specific Antigen) blood
test to detect this cancer in its early stage.

In 1992, Dole again had campaigned hard for his
former rival George Bush, but on November 3, 1992,
Bush lost his bid for reelection to Democrat Bill
Clinton. That same day Dole won his fifth six-year
term to the Senate.

The Republicans, after twelve years of being in
charge of the White House, now watched a
Democratic administration move in. The Democrats
also ruled in the House and Senate. Dole was willing
to cooperate with the new administration if in his
view it advanced the best interests of America.[32] At
that time, Dole's future hopes for the presidency
seemed futile, and he came to terms with staying in
the Senate.

One More Call to Serve

In the spring of 1994, former President Richard M. Nixon—the man who believed Bob Dole would be a good president—died.[1] The eulogy Dole delivered moved many to tears. His remembrance of Nixon's early struggle seemed to parallel his own:

> He [Nixon] was a boy who heard train whistles in the night and dreamed of all the distant places that lay at the end of the track. . . . He was the student who met expenses by doing research at the law library for thirty-five cents an hour, while sharing a rundown farmhouse without water or electricity.

Dole remembered Nixon's maxim: ". . . the greatest sadness is not to try and fail, but to fail to try."

Dole's deep voice faltered as he ended, "May God

Bless Richard Nixon. May God Bless the United States of America."[2]

Several weeks after Nixon's funeral, Dole attended the fiftieth anniversary of the D-Day invasion of Normandy, France. On the plane ride home, Bob Dole thought of the men who had stormed the beaches of Normandy and had made sacrifices for freedom.[3] He thought of their grandchildren and how they deserved to live in a good country.[4] Bob Dole, patriot, war hero,

Dole delivers the eulogy at Nixon's funeral. Nixon's boyhood home is in the background.

and statesman, who had spent almost half his life on Capitol Hill, wondered if he should answer the call to serve his country once more.[5]

A historic event occurred in November 1994. For the first time in forty years, the Republicans took control of both the House and the Senate. Dole resumed his position as majority leader. "The Republicans will have the burden of leadership . . . ," he observed. "If we're the majority, we're going to have to produce."[6] He gained new respect among his colleagues, and in some political circles his name was mentioned as a presidential hopeful.

Dole announced in February 1995, on the *Late Show with David Letterman*, that he was running for president. Dole joked with Letterman, who had introduced Dole as an actual American hero and who displayed a mock campaign button featuring photographs of Dole and Letterman and the slogan "Dole and Dumber." Dole did a takeoff on Letterman's favorite Top Ten list: "We've cut everything thirty percent," Dole quipped. "So I've got a Top Seven list."[7]

Two months after the *Late Show* appearance, Bob Dole returned to Kansas to begin his campaign officially.

> *Wherever I have traveled in this life, I have never forgotten where I came from—or where I go home to. . . . I have come home to Kansas with a grateful heart to declare that I am a candidate for the presidency of the United States.*[8]

Next, he journeyed to his boyhood home of Russell. At a pancake breakfast sponsored by the

Veterans of Foreign Wars, Dole thanked the people of Russell who had always been there for him. It had been over fifty years since he lost the use of his right arm and the town first reached out to him. Once again they presented him with a money-filled cigar box, a symbol of their loyalty and concern.

Former Russell newspaper editor Russ Townsley, who sometimes differed with Dole on the issues, related an incident that occurred in 1976 when Dole entered his first national campaign as Gerald Ford's running mate. A reporter from Boston who came to Russell told Townsley, "I came here to find the skeletons in Bob Dole's closet."

"Let's go look, but you won't find any," Townsley replied. "I've covered every angle I can since 1947, and if there are any, I want to find them too."[9]

Although they did not find any and Townsley has not uncovered any since, Dole had been plagued by image just like other politicians. Critics painted Dole as cold and mean. President Clinton's onetime press secretary Dee Dee Myers called Dole "a very straightforward, snarling attack dog when he wants to be."[10] A Dole senior advisor admitted, "The average person doesn't get to see the likable side of him very often."[11]

As Dole launched his third campaign for the presidency, he received praise—as well as criticism. Some criticized him for flip-flopping on issues during the early phases of the campaign. Some advisors encouraged him to please everybody. Other advisors, including Richard Norton Smith, called themselves

the "Let Dole Be Dole Committee." Smith advised Dole:

> . . . *People expect you to say what's on your mind, not what some consultant or focus group expects to hear . . . a leader is willing to take the long view and to risk short-term unpopularity in pursuit of long-term objectives. He is someone comfortable with himself, sure of his core values. . . . In short, someone very much like you . . .* [12]

Friends and family saw those core values. Republican consultant Mike Murphy commented, "Dole's weakness in politics is that he tells the truth.

Bob Dole, Vice President Al Gore, President Bill Clinton, and Speaker of the House Newt Gingrich engage in serious talks regarding the government shutdown.

And you just can't be punished for that."[13] Sheila
Burke, Dole's chief of staff, insisted, "I have worked
for Dole for eighteen years and I have enjoyed every
minute of it."[14] Elizabeth described her husband as a
"very tender, loving man."[15] Bob's grown daughter,
Robin, who is a therapist for troubled teenagers in
Washington, D.C., agreed. She spent many hours
campaigning for her father, and she still enjoys
spending time with him.

Age became another campaign issue. Bob Dole
would have been seventy-three at his inauguration,
older than anyone ever elected to a first presidential
term. Dole responded to skeptics who believed he did
not have the stamina, "Stick with me for a day and
see for yourself."[16] Some staff members half his age
found it difficult to keep up with their boss's pace.
Dole, the former track star, kept fit by walking briskly
on his treadmill at least twelve miles a week.

Senate colleagues praised Dole for running the
Senate "with sensitivity and craftsmanship."[17] Others
believed that an effective senator does not necessari-
ly make an effective presidential candidate. One
columnist wrote that successful legislators have "to
blur the edges of their positions, bridge gaps with
rivals, let others take credit for their successes."[18] But
good presidential candidates, on the other hand,
must do the opposite and "sharpen their positions,
drive wedges between rivals, take credit for everything."[19]

During the primary campaign, Dole faced his
toughest competition from Lamar Alexander, Pat

Buchanan, and Steve Forbes. After a close win in Iowa and a heartbreaking defeat to Pat Buchanan in New Hampshire, Dole felt like quitting. Then Bob Dole scored a new round of victories in his bid for the Republican nomination after stunning sweeps in March of 1996. After votes were tabulated in California, it was clear that Bob Dole would represent the Republican party in the presidential election against incumbent Bill Clinton.

Dole returned to his job as Senate majority leader. He felt his work would be an asset to the campaign. However, even members of his own party attacked his

The senator posed with Dole for President *staff members Joseph Mason Van Name III, left, and Christopher Little.*

longtime service in the Senate. For them, Dole had become too much of a deal-maker, too much of a compromiser. Dole realized that many people believed that Washington meant deal-making politicians and higher taxes. They identified him with Washington and labeled him a "Washington insider."[20] He was faltering in the polls. After a lot of soul-searching, he decided upon a strategy to breathe life into what some observers saw as a dying campaign.

"The White House or Home"

On May 15, 1996, Bob Dole stunned the nation. In a statement carried live from the Hart Senate Office Building on four major networks, Dole said he was giving up what he dearly loved—his role as majority leader *and* his place in the Senate. He promised to work full-time as a candidate for the presidency of the United States. "And I will then stand before you without office or authority, a private citizen, a Kansan, an American, just a man."[1] His voice wavered. He fought back tears. "I will seek the presidency with nothing to fall back on but the judgment of the people, and nowhere to go but the White House or home."[2]

Views differed regarding his departure. White

nomination for the presidency of the United States, Dole promised less government and reminded listeners that Bob Dole was "the most optimistic man in America."[15]

The convention ended the way Dole had hoped: The delegates left enthusiastic not only about Bob Dole and Jack Kemp, but also about all Republican candidates.[16]

Despite this successful convention, analysts insisted that Dole was engaged in an uphill battle, challenging an incumbent president at a time when unemployment figures were low, profits were high, and consumers were optimistic.[17] Negative ads funded by Democrats paired Dole with Speaker of the House Newt Gingrich, "the cement block attached to Dole's back, dragging him under the water."[18]

Still, Dole's confidence in his ability to be a good president in the final years of the twentieth century did not waver.[19] He promised he could cut taxes by 15 percent and balance the budget. He welcomed people of differing viewpoints into the Republican party. He pointed to the diplomatic experience he had gained traveling the world to deliver America's message of freedom and democracy. "My friends," Dole assured, "I have the experience . . . I am not afraid to lead and I know the way."[20]

During his years on Capitol Hill, Dole worked with eight different presidents. He learned from all the presidents he worked with during his years of government service. Whether they were Republican or Democrat, he recognized their strengths. "I've learned

Bob Dole looks to the future.

a lot from each of them that I could use as president,"
Dole stated on one of his many appearances on NBC-
TV's *Meet the Press.*[21]

However, nothing Bob Dole did or said seemed to
make a difference. Columnist David Broder wrote,
"Bob Dole is a far kinder person, a far better politician
and a far more gifted public servant than the man
most Americans have seen on their TV screens as the
Republican nominee."[22] Some criticized Dole for
wanting to run on past accomplishments. Some said
he lacked a vision and did not have the charisma to
inspire audiences. One Dole campaign official said
that Dole's campaign was off in its strategy, theme,
and message.[23] In late October, when Dole made a
plea to have Ross Perot of the Reform party drop out
of the race, Perot refused. As stories of ethical scan-
dals about the Clinton administration surfaced, Dole
asked the American people over and over, "Where is
the outrage?"[24] but Clinton's popularity remained
high in the polls.

In the final days, the legendary senator's climb
toward the White House was a steep one. Dole earned
the name "Marathon Man."[25] For four days and nights
in a row, he campaigned in nineteen states, hoping
for an upset. He journeyed through different time
zones and weather zones, surviving on forty-five-
minute catnaps. He traveled on planes and buses,
visiting high schools and universities, truck stops,
diners, and a bowling alley in East Lansing, Michigan.
Dole commented, "The last time I fought round the
clock for my country was in 1945 in Italy."[26]

Yet, despite his heroic efforts, the White House

was not his. In the end, Dole won nineteen states and 159 electoral votes and 41 percent of the popular vote. Clinton took thirty-one states and 379 electoral votes—well over the 270 needed to win—and 49 percent of the popular vote.

Dole felt disappointment, but not bitterness or depression. "It's not easy to be a good loser," he said, "but I've tried to conduct myself to let people know there is life after defeat."[27]

Life after defeat meant television appearances on *Saturday Night Live, the Late Show with David Letterman,* and the situation comedy *Suddenly Susan.* On the night of the Super Bowl, he made an appearance on a major credit card commercial, where he quipped, "I just can't win!"[28] He looks forward to the future. He will continue to write letters to children who have had arm injuries, "reaching out to people who may have given up."[29] He will consider law firm offers and public speaking engagements and will continue to speak out on policy issues. But as a private citizen, he'll have time to walk his dog Leader, enjoy a leisurely cup of coffee, reminisce with friends and family, pace longer on his treadmill, listen to music, and whistle a happy tune.

Bob Dole has had a long, distinguished career in public service. His greatness lies in his struggle to survive. His mother's words and the Kansas state motto (*Ad Astra per Aspera*: to the stars through difficulties) still guide him. He survived the bullet that shattered his shoulder and his dreams. He survived prostate cancer. He survived political losses. He remains a powerful force on the American political

scene. In January 1997, President Clinton awarded Dole the Medal of Freedom, the nation's highest civilian honor, a gesture that Dole appreciated.[30] As writer George Gilder stated of Dole, "Triumph, after all, is the message of his own extraordinary life."[31]

Bob Dole could not fulfill his dream of becoming President of the United States, but he is grateful that he had the privilege and the opportunity to run for the office. As a private citizen, he will continue to serve, never forgetting where he started and how many people helped him along the way.

Chronology

1923—Born to Doran and Bina (Talbott) Dole in Russell, Kansas, on July 22.

1941—Graduates from Russell High School and enrolls as a pre-med student at the University of Kansas at Lawrence.

1942—Enlists in the United States Army's Enlisted Reserve Corps.

1943—Called to active duty by the United States Army.

1945—Struck by exploding shell on April 14 that leaves him with a useless right arm.

1948—Marries Phyllis Holden on June 12.

1949—Enrolls at Washburn Municipal College, which later becomes Washburn University, in a joint program for an undergraduate degree in history and a graduate degree in law.

1950—Wins election to the Kansas State Legislature on the Republican ticket (one two-year term) while still in law school.

1952—Earns a Bachelor of Arts in history and a law degree (*magna cum laude*) from Washburn University in Topeka, Kansas; begins his eight-year stint as county attorney.

1954—Birth of his daughter, Robin, on October 18.

1960—After a close primary race, he easily wins the general election to represent Kansas's 6th Congressional District (later renamed the 1st) in the United States Congress.

1964—Votes for the Civil Rights Act; is reelected to Congress in a close race.

1965—Votes for the Voting Rights Act.

1966—Wins another congressional term.

1968—Wins a seat in the United States Senate.

1969—Delivers his first speech on the Senate floor.

1971—Appointed to the chairmanship of the Republican National Committee; tours the nation, speaking for the Republican party.

1972—He and his first wife, Phyllis, divorce.

1973—Eased out of the chairmanship of the Republican National Committee.

1974—Wins a tough Senate reelection fight after Watergate.

1975—Marries Elizabeth Hanford on December 6; his father, Doran, dies.

1976—Becomes Gerald Ford's running mate in the unsuccessful Republican presidential campaign of 1976.

1979—Officially announces his first bid for the presidency of the United States on May 14.

1980—Enters the presidential primary but soon withdraws; wins another term to the United States Senate; becomes Senate Finance Committee chairman.

1982—Leads the fight for TEFRA, the Tax Equity and Fiscal Responsibility Act.

1983—Establishes the Dole Foundation, which finances rehabilitation programs for the mentally and physically handicapped; Bina Dole dies; Dole delivers a eulogy on the Senate floor

for Dr. Hampar Kelikian, the surgeon who performed seven operations on Dole's damaged arm; supports a bill to make Dr. Martin Luther King, Jr.'s birthday a federal holiday.

1984—Elected Senate majority leader.

1985—Leads a senatorial delegation on a trade mission to the Far East in the summer.

1986—Is reelected to his fourth term as a United States Senator; is elected Senate minority leader.

1987—Formally declares his candidacy for the presidential nomination.

1988—Withdraws from the presidential race.

1989—Americans with Disabilities Act (ADA) is passed.

1991—Deals courageously with prostate cancer.

1992—Wins his fifth six-year Senate term.

1994—Delivers eulogy at Richard Nixon's funeral; attends the fiftieth anniversary of the D-Day invasion of Normandy; resumes his position as Senate majority leader.

1995—Announces his candidacy for the presidency of the United States.

1996—Campaigns for the Republican nomination for the presidency for the third time; resigns from the United States Senate; becomes the Republican nominee for the presidency of the United States; is defeated by incumbent Bill Clinton.

1997—Is awarded the Medal of Freedom, the nation's highest civilian honor.

National Political Profile

1961–1969—Serves in the House of Representatives.

1969–1996—Serves in the Senate.

1971–1973—Chairman of the Republican National Committee.

1976—Vice-presidential candidate.

1980–1984—Serves as chairman of the powerful Senate Finance Committee.

1980, 1988, 1996—Seeks Republican nomination for the presidency.

1985–1986, 1995–1996—Serves as Senate majority leader.

1987–1994—Serves as Senate minority leader.

1996—Resigns as senator after thirty-five years of service on Capitol Hill; runs against Bill Clinton for the presidency of the United States; is unsuccessful in his campaign for the presidency.

Chapter Notes

Chapter 1

1. Jake H. Thompson, *Bob Dole: The Republicans' Man for All Seasons* (New York: Fine, 1994), p. 30.

2. Robert Dole and Elizabeth Hanford Dole with Richard Norton Smith, *The Doles: Unlimited Partners* (New York: Simon and Schuster, 1988), p. 49.

3. Ibid., p. 54.

4. Transcript of *60 Minutes* (CBS Television), October 24, 1993, p. 11.

5. Dole and Dole, pp. 58–59.

6. *Congressional Record* (Senate), April 14, 1969, p. 8816.

7. Ibid., p. 8818.

8. Ibid., p. 8821.

9. Thompson, p. 220.

Chapter 2

1. Robert Dole and Elizabeth Hanford Dole with Richard Norton Smith, *The Doles: Unlimited Partners* (New York: Simon and Schuster, 1988), p. 9.

2. Ibid., p. xii.

3. Jake H. Thompson, *Bob Dole: The Republicans' Man for All Seasons* (New York: Fine, 1994), p. 20.

4. Dole and Dole, p. 11.

5. Richard Ben Cramer, *What It Takes* (New York: Vintage Books, 1992), p. 56.

6. Thompson, p. 18.

7. James R. Dickenson, *Home on the Range: A Century on the High Plains* (New York: Scribner, 1995), p. 134.

8. Dole and Dole, p. 15.

Lieutenant Dole

Contents

9. Cramer, p. 43.

10. Dole and Dole, p. 18.

11. Letter from Bub Dawson to the author, October 17, 1995.

12. Thompson, p. 22.

13. Dole and Dole, p. 16.

14. Ibid., p. 19.

15. Thompson, p. 24.

16. Ibid., p. 24.

17. Cramer, p. 58.

18. Dole and Dole, p. 20.

19. Cramer, p. 59.

20. Dole and Dole, p. 16.

21. Cramer, p. 59.

22. Mark Jonathan Harris, *The Homefront: America During World War II* (New York: Putnam, 1984), p. 20.

23. Dole and Dole, p. 21.

24. Ibid.

Chapter 3

1. Robert Dole and Elizabeth Hanford Dole with Richard Norton Smith, *The Doles: Unlimited Partners* (New York: Simon and Schuster, 1988), p. 38.

2. Stanley G. Hilton, *Senator for Sale* (New York: St. Martin's Press, 1995), p. 59.

3. Dole and Dole, p. 42.

4. Ibid.

5. Russell Freedman, *Franklin Delano Roosevelt* (New York: Clarion Books, 1990), p. 170.

6. Richard Ben Cramer, *What It Takes* (New York: Vintage Books, 1992), p. 101.

7. Jake H. Thompson, *Bob Dole: The Republicans' Man for All Seasons* (New York: Fine, 1994), p. 29.

8. Ibid., p. 30.

9. Dole and Dole, p. 44.

10. Debra West, "A Hero Who Saved Face and a Potential President," *The New York Times*, April 15, 1994, p. 8.

11. Noel C. Koch, "Bob Dole Has the Faith to Endure," *The Russell Daily News*, April 13, 1995, no. 87, sec. 2, p. 4, col. 2.

12. Gail Sheehy, "The Whole Robert Dole," *Vanity Fair*, April 1987, p. 114.

13. Mark Jonathan Harris, *The Homefront: America During World War II* (New York: Putnam, 1984), p. 208.

14. Dole and Dole, p. 43.

Chapter 4

1. Transcript of *60 Minutes* (CBS Television), October 24, 1993, p. 10.

2. Richard Ben Cramer, *What It Takes* (New York: Vintage Books, 1992), p. 107.

3. Karen Tumulty, "Lots More Mr. Nice Guy," *Time*, March 13, 1995, p. 76.

4. Robert Dole and Elizabeth Hanford Dole with Richard Norton Smith, *The Doles: Unlimited Partners* (New York: Simon and Schuster, 1988), p. 50.

5. Cramer, p. 132.

6. Ibid., pp. 109, 132.

7. Ibid.

8. Ibid., p. 131.

9. Jake H. Thompson, *Bob Dole: The Republicans' Man for All Seasons* (New York: Fine, 1994), p. 33.

10. Dole and Dole, p. 55.

11. Ibid., p. 52.

12. Cramer, p. 107.

13. Gail Sheehy, "The Whole Robert Dole," *Vanity Fair*, April 1987, p. 113.

14. Cramer, p. 132.

15. Ibid., p. 133.

16. Dole and Dole, p. 53.

17. Cramer, p. 135.

18. Dole and Dole, p. 54.

19. Ibid.

20. Ibid., p. 51

21. Cramer, p. 147.

22. Ibid.

23. Dole and Dole, p. 56.

Chapter 5

1. Transcript of *60 Minutes* (CBS Television), October 24, 1993, p. 11.

2. Charles Moritz, ed., "Robert J(oseph) Dole," *Current Biography* (New York: Wilson, 1987), p. 135.

3. *60 Minutes*, p. 12.

4. Gail Sheehy, "The Whole Robert Dole," *Vanity Fair*, April 1987, p. 117.

5. Robert Dole and Elizabeth Hanford Dole with Richard Norton Smith, *The Doles: Unlimited Partners* (New York: Simon and Schuster, 1988), p. 57.

6. Ibid., p. 58.

7. Ibid.

8. Jake H. Thompson, *Bob Dole: The Republicans' Man for All Seasons* (New York: Fine, 1994), p. 42.

9. Dole and Dole, pp. 17–18.

10. Ibid., p. 97.

11. Thompson, p. 44.

12. Ibid.

13. Dole and Dole, p. 94.

Chapter 6

1. Richard Ben Cramer, *What It Takes* (New York: Vintage Books, 1992), p. 399.

2. Glenn D. Kittler, *Hail to the Chief! The Inauguration Days of Our Presidents* (Philadelphia: Chilton Books, 1965), p. 217.

3. Jake H. Thompson, *Bob Dole: The Republicans' Man for All Seasons* (New York: Fine, 1994), p. 54.

4. Cramer, pp. 395–396.

5. Letter from Bub Dawson to the author, October 17, 1995.

6. Cramer, p. 588.

7. Thompson, p. 54.

8. Campaign leaflet: *Ford/Dole* (The President Ford Committee, James A. Baker, III, chairman, 1976). Courtesy of the Gerald Ford Library.

9. Cramer, p. 400.

10. Ibid., p. 399.

11. Gerald F. Seib and John Harwood, "Dole Is a Main Street Conservative" (staff reporters for *The Wall Street Journal*) in *The Russell Daily News*, April 13, 1995, p. 6.

12. Cramer, p. 587.

13. Robert Dole and Elizabeth Hanford Dole with Richard Norton Smith, *The Doles: Unlimited Partners* (New York: Simon and Schuster, 1988), p. 109.

14. Thompson, p. 54.

15. Dole and Dole, p. 112.

Chapter 7

1. *Congressional Quarterly Almanac*, 92nd Cong., 1st Sess., 1971, vol. 27, p. 283.

2. Jake H. Thompson, *Bob Dole: The Republicans' Man for All Seasons* (New York: Fine, 1994), p. 59.

3. David E. Rosenbaum, "New G.O.P. Chairman," *The New York Times*, Jan. 16, 1971, p. 18.

4. Charles Moritz, ed., "Robert J(oseph) Dole," *Current Biography* (New York: Wilson, 1987), p. 136.

5. Richard Ben Cramer, *What It Takes* (New York: Vintage Books, 1992), p. 599.

6. Rosenbaum, p. 18.

7. Rowland Evans and Robert D. Novak, *Nixon in the White House: The Frustration of Power* (New York: Vintage Books, 1972), p. 363.

8. *Congressional Quarterly Almanac*, 94th Cong., 2nd Sess., 1976, vol. 32, p. 902.

9. Rosenbaum, p. 18.

10. Robert Dole and Elizabeth Hanford Dole with Richard Norton Smith, *The Doles: Unlimited Partners* (New York: Simon and Schuster, 1988), p. 122.

11. J. P. Podolsky, "Robert Dole," *People*, December 13, 1993, p. 123.

12. Dole and Dole, p. 122.

13. "Divorce, Republican Style," *Newsweek*, September 4, 1995, p. 22.

14. Thompson, p. 66.

15. Dole and Dole, p. 122.

16. Eleanora W. Schoenebaum, ed., *Political Profiles: The Nixon/Ford Years* (New York: Facts on File, 1979), p. 174.

17. Dole and Dole, p. 124.

18. Cramer, p. 605.

19. Dole and Dole, p. 127.

20. Ibid., p. 126.

21. Thompson, p. 72.

22. *Congressional Quarterly Almanac*, 94th Cong., 2nd Sess., 1976, vol. 32, p. 902.

23. Ibid.

24. Elizabeth Drew, *Washington Journal: The Events of 1973–74* (New York: Random House, 1974), p. 400.

25. Gerald Ford, *A Time to Heal: The Autobiography of Gerald R. Ford* (New York: Harper and Row, 1979), p. 26.

26. Ibid., p. 177.

27. Dole and Dole, p. 129.

28. Thompson, p. 79.

29. Cramer, pp. 748, 131.

30. Ibid., p. 748.

31. *Live with Regis and Kathie Lee* (ABC Television), July 1, 1996 (live broadcast), 9:00-10:00 A.M. EST.

32. Dole and Dole, pp. 131, 149.

33. Podolsky, p. 123.

34. Edward Klein, "What They're Like at Home," *Parade*, October 15, 1995, p. 5.

35. Carolyn Mulford, *Elizabeth Dole: Public Servant* (Springfield, N.J.: Enslow, 1992), p. 69.

36. Ford, p. 404.

37. Thompson, p. 93.

38. Cramer, p. 756.

39. Thompson, p. 94.

40. Edward L. and Fredrick H. Schapsmeir, *Gerald R. Ford's Date with Destiny* (New York: Lang, 1989), pp. 223–224.

41. Ibid.

42. Transcript of *Meet the Press* (NBC Television), April 16, 1995, p. 13.

43. Thompson, p. 102.

44. Dole and Dole, p. 179.

45. Thompson, pp. 105–106.

46. Ibid., p. 105.

47. Jack W. Germond and Jules Witcover, "Here's Bob," *The Washingtonian*, February 1985, p. 106.

48. Thompson, p. 109.

49. Ibid., p. 110.

Chapter 8

1. Jake H. Thompson, *Bob Dole: The Republicans' Man for All Seasons* (New York: Fine, 1994), p. 114.

2. Robert Dole and Elizabeth Hanford Dole with Richard Norton Smith, *The Doles: Unlimited Partners* (New York: Simon and Schuster, 1988), p. 187.

3. Thompson, p. 118.

4. Richard Ben Cramer, *What It Takes* (New York: Vintage Books, 1992), p. xvii.

5. Dole and Dole, p. 204.

6. Stanley Hilton, *Senator for Sale* (New York: St. Martin's, 1995), p. 125.

7. Jack W. Germond and Jules Witcover, "Here's Bob," *The Washingtonian*, February 1985, p. 109.

8. Rowland Evans and Robert D. Novak, "Bob Dole: New Strongman in the Senate," *Reader's Digest*, March 1995, pp. 186, 192–193.

9. Thompson, p. 127.

10. Evans and Novak, pp. 186–187.

11. Ruth Shalit, "Bob Dole's Vision Thing," *New York Times Magazine*, March 5, 1995, p. 35.

12. Dole and Dole, p. 237.

13. "Bob Dole's Furies," *Newsweek*, November 21, 1988, p. 88.

14. Dole and Dole, p. 244.

15. Hilton, p. 133.

16. "Senate Boss on the Move—A Day With Bob Dole," *U.S. News and World Report*, May 13, 1985, p. 30.

17. Evans and Novak, p. 185.

18. Richard Ben Cramer, *What It Takes* (New York: Vintage Books, 1992), p. 56.

19. Dole and Dole, p. 248.

20. Thompson, p. 155.

21. Hilton, p. 146.

22. "Bob Dole's Furies," pp. 87–89.

23. George Gilder, "Profile: A Loner's Quest," *Life*, September 1987, p. 66.

24. "Bob Dole's Furies," pp. 88.

25. Ibid.

26. Thompson, p. 170.

27. Transcript of *Meet the Press* (NBC Television), April 16, 1995, p. 13.

28. Thompson, p. 170.

29. "The Dole World," *Newsweek*, January 8, 1996, p. 40.

30. Thompson, p. 178.

31. Ibid., p. 205.

32. Ibid., pp. 206–207.

Chapter 9

1. Walter Shapiro, "The Survivor," *Esquire*, April 1995, p. 67.

2. Program from the memorial service of Richard Nixon, April 27, 1994. Courtesy of the Nixon Library.

3. Joe Klein, "They're Back," *Newsweek*, March 6, 1995, p. 26.

4. Terry Golway, "Life in the 90's," *America*, March 11, 1995, p. 4.

5. Karen Tumulty, "Lots More Mr. Nice Guy," *Time*, March 13, 1995, p. 77.

6. *Congressional Quarterly*, "104th Congress: The Senate," Spring 1995, 1st Sess., p. 36.

7. Michael Kramer, "Eyes on the Prize," *Time*, February 13, 1995, p. 24.

8. "Dole Points the Way," *The Russell Daily News*, April 13, 1995, p. 7.

9. Letter from Russell Townsley to the author, November 15, 1995, p. 2.

10. Jake H. Thompson, *Bob Dole: The Republicans' Man for All Seasons* (New York: Fine, 1994), p. 204.

11. "A Hip Dole Gets Out of the Gate," *Newsweek*, February 13, 1995, p. 31.

12. Michael Kramer, "Will the Real Bob Dole Please Stand Up?" *Time*, November 20, 1995, p. 63.

13. Ruth Shalit, "Bob Dole's Vision Thing," *New York Times Magazine*, March 5, 1995, p. 37.

14. "The Most Hated Woman in Politics?" *Glamour*, November 1995, p. 93.

15. Shalit, p. 36.

16. Michael Duffy and Nancy Gibbs, "Facing the Age Issue," *Time*, July 31, 1995, p. 29.

17. "A Taciturn Leader in a Talkative Time," *U.S. News and World Report*, December 18, 1995, p. 39.

18. Steven V. Roberts, "A Warhorse's Toughest Fight," *U.S. News and World Report*, April 10, 1995, p. 45.

19. Ibid.

20. Bob Woodward, *The Choice* (New York: Simon and Schuster, 1996), p. 428.

Chapter 10

1. Richard L. Berke, "Dole Says He Will Leave Senate to Focus on Presidential Race," *The New York Times*, May 16, 1996, p. 1.

2. William Safire, "White House or Home," *The New York Times*, May 16, 1996, p. A25.

3. Richard Stengel, "The Hard Way," *Time*, May 27, 1996, p. 28.

4. R. W. Apple, Jr., "Dole Gamble: Jump Start or Disaster?" *The New York Times*, May 16, 1996, p. B10.

5. Safire, p. A25.

6. Dan Balz, "Dole's Parting Reflections Leave Image of the Core Values of His Career," *The Washington Post*, June 12, 1996, p. A14.

7. "Excerpts From Dole's Speech Offering His Farewell to the Senate," *The New York Times*, June 12, 1996, p. B8.

8. Ted Kopel, *Nightline* (ABC Television), June 11, 1996.

9. Francis X. Clines, "Citizen Dole Bids Farewell to the Senate," *The New York Times*, June 12, 1996, p. B8.

10. *Live with Regis and Kathy Lee*, (ABC Television), July 1, 1996 (live broadcast), 9:00–10:00 A.M. EST.

11. Edward Klien, "What They're Like at Home," *Parade*, October 15, 1995, p. 5.

12. "Economic Elixir or Voodoo Economics?" *U.S. News and World Report*, August 19, 1996, p. 38.

13. "'General' Acclaim For GOP's Dole," *The New York Post*, August 13, 1996, p. 2.

14. "Susan Taps Into Mother Lode of Hope," *The New York Post*, August 14, 1996, p. 2.

15. Richard L. Berke, "Candidate Says He Will Lead Diverse, 'Inclusive' GOP," *The New York Times*, August 16, 1996, p. 1.

16. Jerelyn Eddings and Michael Barone with Linda Kulman, "Eyes on the Prize," *U.S. News and World Report*, August 19, 1996, p. 30.

17. Robert J. Samuelson, "The Message From 1896?" *Newsweek*, August 12, 1996, p. 51.

18. Jack Newfield, "Why Dole Can't Connect," *The New York Post,* October 9, 1996, p. 16.

19. Transcript of *Meet the Press* (NBC Television), April 16, 1995, p. 10.

20. Transcript of *CBS Evening News* (CBS Television), April 10, 1995, p. 1.

21. *Meet the Press,* p. 10.

22. David Broder, "Dole Never Recognized His Limitations," *The New York Post,* November 3, 1996, p. 55.

23. Jake Thompson, "Consultant: Dole's Campaign 'Worst'; Miscues Recounted," *The Kansas City Star,* reprinted in *The Scranton Times,* November 11, 1996, p. 11.

24. Daily News Washington Bureau, "Dole Shreds Media," *The Daily News,* October 26, 1996, p. 6.

25. Steve Dunleavy, "Marathon Man," *The New York Post,* November 3, 1996, p. 6.

26. "Campaign Etc.," *Philadelphia Daily News,* November 1, 1996, p. 8.

27. *Today* show interview with correspondent Lisa Myers (NBC Television), February 3, 1997 (live broadcast).

28. Visa commercial shown during the second quarter of the Super Bowl, January 26, 1997.

29. "The Clintons and the Doles: Exclusive *LHJ* Interviews," *Ladies' Home Journal,* November 1996, p. 176.

30. *Today* show, February 3, 1997.

31. George Gilder, "A Loner's Quest," *Life,* September 1987, p. 66.

Further Reading

Books

Barone, Michael. *The Almanac of American Politics.* Washington: National Journal, 1994.

Cramer, Richard Ben. *Bob Dole.* New York: Vintage Books, 1995.

———. *What It Takes.* New York: Vintage Books, 1992.

Dole, Robert, edited by Wendy Wolff and Richard A. Baker. *Historical Almanac of the United States Senate: A Series of Bicentennial Minutes Presented to the Senate During the One Hundredth Congress.* Washington: U.S. Government Printing Office (A U.S. Senate bicentennial publication. Senate Document 100-35. 100th Cong., 2nd Sess.), 1989.

Dole, Robert, and Elizabeth Hanford Dole, with Richard Norton Smith. *The Doles: Unlimited Partners.* New York: Simon and Schuster, 1988. (Re-released in 1996 with several additional chapters.)

Ford, Gerald. *A Time to Heal: The Autobiography of Gerald R. Ford.* New York: Harper and Row, 1979.

Harris, Mark Jonathan. *The Homefront: America During World War II.* New York: Putnam, 1984.

Hilton, Stanley G. *Senator for Sale.* New York: St. Martin's Press, 1995.

Mulford, Carolyn. *Elizabeth Dole: Public Servant.* Hillside, N.J.: Enslow Publishers, 1992.

Thompson, Jake H. *Bob Dole: The Republicans' Man for All Seasons.* New York: Fine, 1994.

Wellman, Mark, and John Flin. *Climbing Back.* Waco, Tex.: WRS Publishing, 1992.

Woodward, Bob. *The Choice.* New York: Simon and Schuster, 1996.

Magazines

Eddings, Jerelyn and Michael Barone with Linda Kulman, "Eyes on the Prize," *U.S. News and World Report,* August 10, 1996, pp. 22–35.

Fineman, Howard. "Just the Ticket?" *Newsweek,* August 19, 1996, pp. 23–27.

Gilder, George. "A Loner's Quest." *Life,* September 1987, pp. 63–66.

Roberts, Steven. "A Warhorse's Toughest Fight." *U.S. News and World Report,* April 10, 1995, pp. 40, 45.

Podolsky, J. P. "Robert Dole." *People,* December 13, 1993, pp. 120–123.

Shalit, Ruth. "Bob Dole's Vision Thing." *The New York Times Magazine,* March 5, 1995, pp. 32ff.

Shapiro, Walter. "The Survivor." *Esquire,* April 1995, pp. 65–67.

Stengel, Richard. "The Hard Way." *Time,* May 27, 1996, pp. 22–28.

Index